OSBERT T

"Wry and unexpected, it offers exaggerated villains, elaborate murders, twists and narrow escapes."

SUNDAY TIMES

"Fans of Roald Dahl and Chris Priestley will savour every gruesome drop of this stylish, grisly and original comedy."

THE TIMES

"A riveting story – a clever mix of humour with some very dark and gruesome moments and a couple of real shocks towards the end."

PRIMARY TIMES

"Bloodthirsty and mysterious with a sharp spike in its tail, Osbert's story is a deliciously dark invitation to the strange world of Schwartzgarten, a city corrupt with shadows and secrets – and in need of a hero."

WE LOVE THIS BOOK

"A macabre tale full of ghoulish and gruesome escapades. A frightening but appealing anti-hero."

BOOKTRUST

"Macabre and gruesome and wickedly funny."

For Jo, who knows the hidden dangers

of cloisonné peacocks.

ORCHARD BOOKS
338 Euston Road, London NW1 3BH
Orchard Books Australia
Level 17/207 Kent Street, Sydney, NSW 2000

ISBN 978 1 40831 456 2

First published in Great Britain in 2013
This paperback edition published in 2014
Text © Christopher William Hill 2013

A CIP catalogue record for this book is available from the British
Library.

10 9 8 7 6 5 4 3 2 1

Printed in Great Britain

Orchard Books is a division of Hachette Children's Books, an
Hachette UK company.

www.hachette.co.uk

Schwartzgarten map illustration by Artful Doodlers © Orchard Books 2013
The Informant illustrations © Chris Naylor 2013

TALES FROM
HWARTZGARTEN

THE
WOEBEGONE
TWINS

Christopher William Hill

ORCHARD

THE CITY OF SCHWARTZGARTEN

CEMETERY

V. Bone · Orchard Street

OLD TOWN

N

W   E

S

1. Poisoner's Row
2. Borgburg Avenue
3. Mr Lomm's School
4. Schwartzgarten Museum
5. Bildstein and Bildstein
6. Olga Van Veenen's House
7. Schwartzgarten Bookshop
8. Governor's Palace
9. Grand Duke Augustus Bridge
10. Department of Police
11. Glue Factory
12. Anheim Street
13. Aunt Gisela's House
14. Donmerplatz
15. Mrs Moritz's Shop
16. Cinema of Blood
17. Zoological Gardens

CHAPTER ONE

The Mortenberg twins stared out from the window of Aunt Gisela's kitchen. A man peered back at them, his piercing black eyes hooded by heavy grey lids. His head was unusually round and his skin had a wax-like pallor rarely seen on the face of a living creature.

'He's come to kill us,' whispered Feliks.

'Probably,' replied Greta. 'He looks the type that might.'

It was not unusual for the twins to expect the worst, nor was it entirely wrong for them to do so. From their earliest days they had been known as the Woebegone Twins, abandoned to their fate by disagreeable parents who preferred holidays in exotic climes and super-fast motor cars to spending time with their unfortunate offspring. Had it not been for Aunt Gisela, who had adopted the twins, they would have been brought up warped and peculiar within the foreboding walls of the Schwartzgarten Reformatory for Maladjusted Children. Sometimes it is kinder to lie than to tell the truth, and

Aunt Gisela had told the twins that their parents had died tragically in mysterious circumstances.

So the Woebegone Twins lived in Schwartzgarten with their aunt and her pet parrot, Karloff, in a warm and cheerful house in the grimmest, darkest part of the Old Town. When money was plentiful, Aunt Gisela would bake spiced gingerbread and her famous vanilla pudding. When times were hard, she would switch off the lights and sit inside her kitchen cupboard with the twins in her arms, hiding from the bailiffs.

The house always smelt of baking and beeswax and the aroma of oil of petunia, which Aunt Gisela dabbed liberally behind her ears every morning 'to keep away the moths'.

The twins had healthy appetites for the food that Aunt Gisela prepared for them. But there was one thing and one thing alone that they could not eat, and that thing was the humble almond nut. It was a discovery made early in their lives, when Aunt Gisela set to work baking the twins an almond marzipan torte on the occasion of their fifth birthdays. It was perhaps the most beautiful thing she had ever concocted; a towering confection of almond sponge cake with layers of almond marzipan and cloudberry jam, topped with glittering shards of almond nougatine.

'Eat up,' urged Aunt Gisela. 'You can eat the whole cake if you want, my hungry little monsters.'

The effect was instantaneous and dramatic. As soon as the twins sank their teeth into the moist, plump slices of almond cake their tongues began to swell. And swell. And swell.

'Well, I wasn't expecting that,' said Aunt Gisela, telephoning for the doctor.

When Doctor Lempick arrived he examined the twins carefully. They were both deathly pale, and their tongues lolled from their mouths like deflated helium balloons.

'What I want to know is this,' said Aunt Gisela, 'what's happened to their tongues and will they be like it forever?'

Doctor Lempick smiled and shook his head. 'They are allergic to almond nuts,' he concluded. 'Their tongues will return to the normal size in due course. But please, never ever feed them another almond as long as they live.'

Apart from an allergy to almonds and the unfortunate disappearance of their parents, it would have seemed to the casual observer that the Mortenberg twins were entirely unremarkable. The only point of note was the striking similarity between the two children, although Greta was a little shorter and slightly stronger than her brother Feliks. Their hair was deep red, the colour of burnt barley sugar, and their pale faces were liberally scattered with freckles, but this hardly marked them out as extraordinary. If anything, it was Aunt Gisela who attracted most attention as she bustled along the cobbled streets of the Old Town with the twins in tow. Passers-by would often stop and stare at the woman, smiling with admiration and nodding as if at a fondly recalled memory.

'What are you staring at?' Aunt Gisela would shout, shaking her fist. 'Nothing better to do than gawp at old women who've done you no wrong?'

And though the twins often asked their aunt why she bawled and screamed at strangers in the street, she seemed deliberately vague on the subject.

Aunt Gisela's behaviour was curious at times, but her love for the twins was beyond doubt. So Greta and Feliks were happy to let their beloved aunt scream at whomsoever she wanted and were grateful for a roof over their heads.

But as the twins reached their eleventh birthdays,

money was short and getting shorter and Aunt Gisela had no choice but to advertise for a boarder to rent a spare room in the house. And it was this boarder who now peered in through the window at the twins.

'That's him,' said Aunt Gisela. 'Our new houseguest! Mr Morbide!'

She ran to the door and opened it wide.

'Mr Morbide!' cried Karloff from his cage. 'Mr Morbide!'

Morbide entered. He was a tall and bulky man and had to stoop his head beneath the lintel. He was cloaked in a long black overcoat and carried a large suitcase and a small leather bag.

'Come in, come in!' cried Aunt Gisela, giving the man a sly wink as she led him into the kitchen.

'Good evening,' growled Morbide in a voice so low that the teacups trembled in the rack above the sink.

The Woebegone Twins gasped and took a step backwards.

Feliks was quite certain that he saw a beetle drop from inside the man's overcoat and scuttle off across the tiled floor.

'Pull up a chair and eat,' commanded Aunt Gisela, grabbing a pan from the stove. 'Eat.'

Morbide sat at the table but did not remove his coat. The twins stared hard at the man, who stared back at them and grunted. He reached into his pocket and retrieved a calling card, which he slid across the table to Greta. The name Morbide was embossed on the card, as if written in dripping blood.

'Well, sit down you two,' barked Aunt Gisela cheerfully. 'Duck eggs all round!'

The twins did as they were told and sat, hardly daring to breathe. They ate in silence.

One thing seemed certain to Greta; Morbide had murder on his mind.

<hr />

Aunt Gisela stood in the kitchen after supper, washing dishes and puffing away on a stubby De Keyser cigar as Morbide nursed a glass of cherry schnapps. Karloff squawked in his cage, whistling and screaming intermittently.

'Stop that now,' said Aunt Gisela, pulling the cloth over the cage. 'I can't hear myself think.'

The twins carried out their chores in silence; Feliks wiped down the kitchen table as Greta swept the floor. One thought and one thought alone occupied their minds – why had Aunt Gisela allowed a murderous maniac to lodge with them?

As soon as Morbide had left the room the question bubbled up like soda water in a shaken bottle.

'Why did you let him in?' demanded Greta. 'Why did he have to come to live here with us?'

Aunt Gisela took a sip of apple brandy, which she swilled round her mouth, gargled and swallowed.

'Morbide's last landlady choked to death on a plum stone, leaving the poor man without a home,' she mumbled.

'At least that's what he says,' whispered Greta, who had formulated an entirely different explanation.

Aunt Gisela stared at her. 'What do you mean, child?'

'I mean,' said Greta, 'his landlady's probably lying dead in a pool of blood somewhere.'

Feliks nodded in agreement. His sister's conclusion chimed perfectly with his own assessment of the situation.

'Maybe he's come to kill us as well,' he added as they heard Morbide moving heavily in the room above.

'Then you'll be sorry, Aunt Gisela,' said Greta, 'sorry that you didn't believe us.'

'Oh, he won't kill you,' said Aunt Gisela, puffing hard on her cigar, her eyes burning brightly through the fog of smoke. 'Because he knows that if he does, I'll kill him right back.'

───◆───

The next evening, Greta watched as Morbide adjusted his coat and top hat in front of the hall mirror. He nodded goodbye, opened the front door and set off along the darkened street. Greta waited until the lodger had disappeared from view, then ran back into the kitchen.

'Come on,' she said.

'Where?' asked Feliks, looking up from one of Aunt Gisela's recipe books.

'To look for clues,' said Greta, pulling her brother by the arm and almost dragging him up the stairs to Morbide's bedroom. She tried the handle but the door was locked.

'So, that's it,' said Feliks in relief, turning back towards the stairs. 'We can't investigate after all.'

'Not so fast,' said Greta, seizing Feliks by the sleeve of

his pullover. She reached into her pocket. 'I've got Aunt Gisela's spare key.'

'What if he comes back?' asked Feliks.

'He'll be gone for hours most probably,' said Greta as she turned the key in the lock. 'We've got the whole place to ourselves.'

'I wish Aunt Gisela was here,' said Feliks.

'She took Karloff and went out to buy cigars,' said Greta. 'At least, that's what Morbide says.'

She turned the handle and the door creaked open. The curtains were closed; Morbide's bedroom was in darkness. Greta switched on the light. It was not a large room, but it was tidily kept. The bed was made and the pillows had been neatly plumped. There was a jug on the washstand and a bar of soap in a dish. Morbide's suitcase and leather bag stood on a table beside the fireplace. Greta sighed: there were no obvious clues to be seen. She knelt on the floor and reached beneath the bed.

'What are you doing?' whispered Feliks, hardly daring to set foot in the bedroom.

'If I was a murderer,' said Greta, 'I'd hide all my murdering tools under here.' Her hands grasped a large cardboard box, which she pulled out from under the bed. She lifted the lid.

'What's wrong?' asked Feliks, as any remaining trace of colour seemed to drain from his sister's face. He took a tentative step into the room.

Silently, and with trembling hands, Greta held out the box to her brother and Feliks peered inside. There, staring back at him with motionless eyes, was the head of Aunt Gisela.

'He's murdered her,' he whispered hoarsely. 'He's killed Aunt Gisela.'

No sooner had the words formed on the boy's lips than a creak could be heard on the staircase.

Morbide had returned home.

CHAPTER TWO

There was no escape. Greta and Feliks backed further into the room as Morbide reached the top of the stairs and lumbered forward through the open doorway, glowering at the twins as he did so.

'That's mine, I think,' said Morbide, lifting the cardboard box containing Aunt Gisela's decapitated head from Feliks's outstretched arms. He stooped to return the head to its resting place beneath the bed.

'Don't come any closer,' said Greta.

'Or what?' asked Morbide, as a faint hint of amusement played across his lips.

'Or I'll scream,' replied Greta.

The smile that had been threatening to form on Morbide's face finally erupted. 'You'll scream?' he echoed. 'You think that scares me?' He took another step towards the twins and opened his mouth wide to reveal a set of fangs, as sharp as needles.

'A vampire!' gasped Greta.

'Vampires don't exist,' said Feliks, pinching his arm

to make quite sure he wasn't dreaming, then wishing desperately that he was.

'I hate to contradict the young,' said Morbide, removing his top hat and making a polite bow of his head. 'But I can confidently assure you that vampires most certainly do exist.'

Greta threw back her head and opened her mouth wide.

'She warned you,' shouted Feliks defiantly, as his sister screamed with such ferocity that the jug rattled on Morbide's washstand and the floorboards shuddered beneath them.

Morbide stared open-mouthed at the girl. A dog barked in terror from the house next door, and there was a sharp blast of a police whistle in the street outside. Morbide turned, uncertainly.

'Don't scream again,' he whispered nervously, clasping his hands together in a plea for silence.

'Or what?' asked Greta, standing her ground. 'Are you going to chop us into pieces and bury us under the floorboards?'

'An intriguing suggestion,' said Morbide. 'But not today, I think.'

Greta opened her mouth and prepared to scream again.

'It was a joke,' said Morbide, waving his hands desperately. 'I was joking.'

Downstairs, there was a loud knock. Morbide closed the bedroom door and leaned against it, barring the way out.

'If you don't let us go, I *will* scream again,' said Greta.

'Then they'll break in and arrest you,' said Feliks.

'Or stab you in the heart with a wooden stake and turn you to dust,' added Greta.

Morbide hesitated. He opened the door and stepped out onto the landing. Slowly, he made his way down the staircase, removing his vampire fangs and burying them deep in the pocket of his overcoat. He unlocked the door and opened it a crack. A police constable stood outside.

'Yes?' said Morbide, gazing at the floor and trying his hardest to appear nonchalant.

'I've got ears, haven't I?' said the constable, pushing his way into the hall and closing the door behind him. 'I heard screaming.'

'Arrest him!' cried Greta, running down the stairs.

'Not so quick,' shouted the constable. 'You'll slip and break your neck, and then there'll be forms to fill in.'

'He's trying to kill us,' insisted Feliks, following Greta downstairs into the hall.

The constable raised his eyebrows at Morbide. 'That's children, isn't it?' he said. 'Always thinking the worst of adults.' He stared hard at Morbide. 'Have we met before?'

'I don't think so,' replied Morbide.

'Just got one of those faces, haven't you?' said the constable.

'I suppose I must have,' said Morbide. A silence hung uneasily and Morbide attempted a smile. 'There's been a misunderstanding,' he said at last.

'There hasn't been a misunderstanding,' said Greta, tugging at the constable's sleeve. 'He's got fangs!'

Morbide gave a broad smile to reveal that this was no longer the case and Greta blinked.

'He's got Aunt Gisela's head in a box,' said Feliks. 'It's under his bed. Go up and look if you don't believe us.'

'Well, this is irregular,' said the constable, who considered backing out through the front door and pretending he had never arrived in the first place. Children screaming, that was one thing, but heads in boxes concealed beneath beds; that was something different altogether. He made a note in his pocketbook.

'Head, one. Human.' He looked up. 'Big head, small head?'

'What *size*?' gasped Greta.

'Big or small head?' repeated the constable.

'Aunt Gisela-sized,' said Feliks.

The constable continued to scrawl in his book. 'Adult head. In box. Concealed beneath bed.' He paused. 'What sort of bed?'

'It doesn't matter what sort of bed,' said Greta.

'It might,' said the constable defensively.

'Aren't you going to do anything?' begged Feliks.

'What's the hurry?' asked the constable, remembering well the maxim, He who acts quickest is sorry soonest. 'The head's not going anywhere, is it?'

Suddenly, the front door was flung open.

'They were all out of De Keyser cigars,' said Aunt Gisela, entering the hall with Karloff on her shoulder and bustling through to the kitchen. 'I had to get foreign.'

Greta screamed and Morbide clutched his hands to his ears.

'Aunt Gisela?' mumbled Feliks in disbelief.

The twins followed Aunt Gisela into the kitchen, the constable trailing cautiously behind.

'What's all the screaming for?' said Aunt Gisela. 'You're worse than the parrot.'

'Worse than the parrot!' squawked Karloff. 'Worse than the parrot!'

'Seems she's made a miraculous recovery,' said the constable with a grin. 'Decapitated one minute, whole again the next.'

'Who's he?' demanded Aunt Gisela, jerking her head in the constable's direction.

'Police,' said the constable.

'Got a match?' asked Aunt Gisela, biting the end off a cigar and spitting it into the sink.

'I haven't,' said the constable.

'What good are the police anyway?' said Aunt Gisela, leaning over to light the cigar from the stove. She put a pan on the ring and poured in a glug of oil, all the time puffing great clouds of suffocating grey cigar smoke.

The constable shifted uneasily. 'I suppose if she's not been murdered, there's not much sense me being here.'

'Murdered?' cackled Aunt Gisela. 'Who told you I'd

been murdered?'

'We did,' said Greta, still eyeing Morbide with suspicion.

The constable inched his way to the door.

'Well, go if you're going,' said Aunt Gisela.

Morbide showed the constable into the hall. As soon as they were out of earshot, Aunt Gisela turned to the twins. 'Now what's all this about murders?'

'What do you really know about Morbide?' whispered Greta urgently.

Aunt Gisela shrugged her shoulders and cracked four duck eggs into the hissing pan. 'I know he pays his rent, what more can I ask of the man?'

'You can ask him not to be a murderer,' said Feliks.

'Why's it always got to be murderers?' said Aunt Gisela. 'Once in a while it might be nice for you to think that people are burglars or kidnappers. But no, it's always murderers.' She took a spatula and flicked hot fat over the eggs, watching as the bright yellow yolks grew cloudy.

'But Morbide *is* a murderer,' insisted Greta. 'And he wants to kill us.'

'Kill you?' barked Aunt Gisela, tossing in a veal steak,

which hissed and spat in the pan.

'And he wants to drink our blood, probably,' added Feliks.

'Kill you!' squawked Karloff. 'drink our blood!'

'Why would he want to kill you?' said Aunt Gisela, wiping beads of sweat from her brow. 'That's what I'm asking you. Why?'

'Because we know his deep dark secret,' said Greta earnestly. 'He's a vampire!'

Aunt Gisela threw back her head and laughed, a thunderous noise so loud that Karloff moved from foot to foot on his perch, screaming, 'Police! Police! Murder!'

Aunt Gisela was still cackling with laughter as Morbide returned from seeing the constable out. Greta and Feliks watched his every move.

'I think I'll go up to my room now,' said Morbide.

'You won't,' said Aunt Gisela, pronging the veal steak with a fork and flipping it from the sizzling pan and onto a plate. 'You'll stay and eat. The twins think you're a vampire. They think you want to murder them.'

'Me?' said Morbide. 'Murder them?'

'That's what I said,' crowed Aunt Gisela. 'No sense

in it, I said.' She turned to the twins and grinned. 'If he wanted to drink the blood of children, don't you think he would have found a house with plumper, rosier-cheeked children to choose from?'

Morbide gave the twins a twinkling smile.

'Show Aunt Gisela what's in the box you hide under your bed,' shouted Greta defiantly.

'Very well,' replied Morbide quietly, lumbering from the room and climbing the stairs. He returned moments later with the box under his arm. 'For you, Gisela,' he said. 'I had Duttlinger make it for me.'

Aunt Gisela took the box and lifted the lid. She stared inside and the glass eyes of the lifeless wax head stared back at her. But she did not faint with shock as Greta had secretly predicted.

'I had a wax head,' murmured Aunt Gisela, her eyes moistening. 'But it was lost. All those years ago.' She stubbed out her cigar in a saucer and turned to Greta and Feliks. 'There are some things you need to know,' she said, lighting a fresh cigar, 'and it's about time you knew them. Pour yourselves a glass of lingonberry cordial and eat your eggs and we'll talk things over.'

The twins sat at the table, their eyes firmly fixed on their aunt's lodger.

'Morbide's not a danger to anyone,' said Aunt Gisela, puffing hard on her cigar. 'He's an actor.'

Morbide smiled awkwardly, and took his seat.

'An actor?' said Feliks, sensing, with embarrassment, the beginnings of a satisfactory explanation.

Aunt Gisela opened the door of a high cupboard and took down a faded photograph album. She turned the pages and held out the book to the twins.

'There,' she said. 'You see?'

She pointed at a newspaper cutting from the front page of *The Informant*, which had grown yellow with age. The twins stared hard at the brittle paper. Beneath the headline 'Gisela Announces Retirement' was a photograph of their aunt. Not the Aunt Gisela they had known all their lives, but a very different, younger Aunt Gisela, with a soft round face and eyes so warm they could have melted ice.

It was the most beautiful face Greta and Feliks had ever seen.

'I was gorgeous then,' said Aunt Gisela, who didn't

have a proud bone in her body. It was simply a statement of fact.

'That's really you?' asked Greta.

Aunt Gisela laughed and nodded.

'But that was twenty years ago,' she said.

'Who's that?' asked Feliks, pointing at a boy who stood beside Aunt Gisela in the photograph, holding a wax head in his hands.

'That's me,' said Morbide. 'Or at least, it was.'

Aunt Gisela smiled fondly. 'And that's my wax head he's clutching, bless the boy.'

'*The Demon Decapitator*,' said Greta, reading from a note beneath the cutting, written in her aunt's hand.

'Last movie we ever made together,' said Aunt Gisela. 'A mad axeman was on the loose, and he cut off my head,' she cackled. 'Oh, the laughs we had. And the blood!'

'The place was awash with blood,' agreed Morbide, beating his fist against the table as he convulsed with laughter.

The food went uneaten and the lingonberry cordial remained undrunk as the twins struggled to make sense of all that they were hearing.

'You were an actress?' said Feliks.

Aunt Gisela smiled and nodded her head. 'A long time ago, when the world was young,' she said, turning the page of the album and revealing a large studio portrait of her younger self, wearing fangs and a long, black wig.

'But you look so tall,' said Feliks.

'The older you get, the more your bones shrink and shrivel,' said Aunt Gisela, running her finger nostalgically over the faded photograph.

'But why did you stop acting in movies?' asked Greta.

'Because I wasn't slim and pale any more,' sighed Aunt Gisela. 'It was a shattering shock.'

'She was like a mother to me,' said Morbide, clutching Aunt Gisela's tiny hand and giving it a gentle squeeze.

'Better than a mother,' corrected Aunt Gisela. 'That's what you used to say. That I was better than a mother.'

'And that's why people stop and stare at you in the street,' said Greta, piecing the clues together in her mind, 'because they recognise you from the movies you made?'

'Well, it's not for my looks now, is it?' Aunt Gisela took another puff on her cigar. 'I'm flesh and blood like the rest of them. Nothing special about me.'

Greta frowned. 'Were you ever going to tell us?'

'Don't know,' said Aunt Gisela. 'I hadn't thought that far.'

'You said nothing much happened in your life until we came along,' said Greta, annoyed with herself for believing that a remarkable aunt could ever have led an unremarkable existence.

'What did happen to our parents?' asked Feliks, suddenly doubting everything he had ever been told.

'You've got to tell us now,' said Greta.

'They ran away,' said Aunt Gisela. 'I wish I could say they didn't, but they did.'

There was a long silence as this information slowly sank in.

'But why did they run away?' asked Feliks at last.

Aunt Gisela took a deep breath. It was a hard truth to tell. 'They didn't like the look of you,' she said. 'And so you came to live with me. And I gave you all the love in the world. It was a long time after I'd given up on movies. I'd turned my back on that way of things.'

'So our parents aren't really dead after all?' said Greta.

'Oh, they're dead all right,' replied Aunt Gisela. 'At

least they are now. Died in a motoring accident when you were just babes in arms. And good riddance to them, I say. Selfish wolves, they were.' She closed the album. 'Put on your warm clothes, we're going out.'

Greta and Feliks ran upstairs to their rooms, put on their coats and gloves and returned to the kitchen. Aunt Gisela had changed into a black cape and as she smiled at the twins, she revealed her own set of fangs. Morbide picked up his top hat.

'Where are you taking us?' asked Feliks.

'To the Cinema of Blood,' said Aunt Gisela, putting Karloff back in his cage. 'It's as well that you know the whole truth.'

CHAPTER THREE

——◆•×•◆——

The Cinema of Blood was situated in the darkest, most westerly corner of Schwartzgarten, close to the cemetery gates, in a district known by many as Death's Doorstep.

'It's a bad neighbourhood,' said Aunt Gisela, holding the twins close to her as they wound their way through the Old Town, passing bars and cafés that reeked of brandy and cigarette smoke. They were safe of course; nobody would approach them with Morbide following behind.

Rounding a corner, they entered the very heart of Death's Doorstep. The buildings were grey and crumbling, and the shops that once lined the streets had closed down, their windows shuttered. The cinema was reached by way of a narrow alleyway leading past the high walls of ancient hotels, and large peeling advertising hoardings for schnapps and liver pills. There before them loomed the Cinema of Blood.

The outer walls of the cinema had been carved to resemble the face of a hideous gargoyle, peering out diabolically from the street corner. The eyes were painted white, but the passage of time had yellowed them. The entrance into the cinema was through a mouth-shaped doorway, beneath a set of sharply pointed fangs, painted to look as though they were dripping with scarlet blood.

The cinema was plastered with faded and torn posters, all decorated with stomach-churning images of murder and mayhem: *The Bloodied Handkerchief, The Curse of the Blind Butcher,* and *The Night of a Thousand Fangs,* which, as Morbide explained, was a blood-chilling movie about a particularly unlucky dentist who was pursued along darkened streets by five hundred vampires.

A small kiosk stood just inside the entrance to the cinema, beside which a new poster had been pasted: *Dollman.*

A doctor with a stethoscope and a complexion as grey as the grave glared out from the poster through penetrating green eyes. Greta could feel her spine tingling as she read the words: 'The creatures are coming…'

Feliks shuddered and Greta laughed and poked him in the ribs.

'Gisela?' said the woman in the kiosk. 'Is that really you?'

'It's me all right,' said Aunt Gisela. 'Greta, Feliks, this is my old friend Mrs Moritz.'

The woman beamed at the twins from behind her wire mesh screen. 'Come to be terrified, have you?'

'They have,' said Aunt Gisela. 'Four tickets for *Dollman* and two bags of chocolate skulls.'

Mrs Moritz slid the tickets across the copper counter and passed two paper bags to the twins.

'How's Mr Moritz?' asked Aunt Gisela.

'Tucked up safe and warm where he belongs,' said Mrs Moritz. 'Schwartzgarten Municipal Cemetery.'

Aunt Gisela cackled and Mrs Moritz cackled back.

Feliks took out a chocolate skull and held it between his thumb and forefinger.

'You have to squeeze them hard,' said Aunt Gisela. 'That's the way to get the stuff out.'

Feliks squeezed the skull and a trickle of lingonberry-flavoured blood oozed out from inside.

'What happens in the movie?' asked Greta, taking out a handful of the skulls and squeezing them into a bloodied pulp.

'It's about a mad doctor called Kessler,' said Morbide. He tapped the side of his head with a stumpy finger. 'Gone completely cuckoo from breathing in all the chemicals in his laboratory. And he digs up corpses and carts them back to his laboratory in a motor hearse.'

'Why?' asked Feliks.

'To reanimate them, of course,' said Morbide. 'Like an army of living dolls. I won't tell you any more. You'll have to wait and see.'

Cockroaches darted across the carpeted floor as they took their seats in the cinema's darkened auditorium, which was lit only by flickering electric bulbs to suggest candlelight. The air was heavy with the musty smell of stale cigar smoke, which had sunk deep into the plush red velvet upholstery. Though the cinema was half-empty, an appreciative murmur soon passed around the audience as Morbide and Aunt Gisela were recognised. Greta and Feliks sat breathless with excitement.

'Whatever happens, don't be frightened,' said Aunt Gisela in a hushed voice. 'There are no real monsters or walking corpses. It's just pretend. Don't ever forget that. Not even for a minute,' she added, rubbing her hands together and sitting forward in her seat.

It was a silent film, so Mrs Moritz had hurried through

from the kiosk to sit at the piano at the very front of the auditorium, hammering away loudly as the cinema screen flickered into life.

The twins settled back into their seats. A caption was projected on the screen.

IN THE LABORATORY OF DOCTOR KESSLER.

Doctor Kessler appeared on screen, wearing a long white laboratory coat and a black bow tie. He clutched a test tube in a gloved hand, as experiments bubbled and smoked in the laboratory behind him. A motionless figure lay on a bench, covered by a sheet.

'There's one of the corpses he's going to reanimate!' whispered Morbide with obvious relish. 'One flick of that lever and the body will come back to life!'

As if responding to Morbide's observation, Doctor Kessler pulled the lever and a spark of electricity crackled through his laboratory. And as the electricity sparked on the screen, so too did the seats of the auditorium – bright flashes of blue that rippled from row to row. Aunt Gisela shrieked and Feliks and Greta jolted so much they spilt their chocolate skulls on the carpet, where they were carried off into the darkness by a surging army of cockroaches.

'That's Von Merhart's doing,' explained Morbide, placing his hand gently on Aunt Gisela's arm. 'The seats were wired up on his orders.' He turned to the twins. 'Von Merhart owns the movie studio. He's always looking for new ways to terrify his audience.'

'Curse the man,' muttered Aunt Gisela, as another jolt of electricity knocked the cigar from her mouth and on to her lap, where it singed her cape. 'He could give an old woman a heart attack.'

On the screen, the reanimated corpse staggered to its feet, its arms outstretched. Doctor Kessler's eyes glittered with pure malevolence.

'That's me,' whispered Morbide, pointing to the screen as Doctor Kessler's assistant arrived, carrying in his arms another corpse.

It was almost impossible to recognise Morbide. His back was hunched and he was disguised by a shock of black hair and enormous teeth with receding gums.

'My trademark,' whispered Morbide proudly. 'A humped back!'

Every time Doctor Kessler reanimated a corpse, the

seats in the auditorium pulsed with electricity. It seemed that Doctor Kessler was endlessly reanimating corpses. Aunt Gisela frowned and sat unimpressed with her arms folded, chewing at the end of her cigar. She did not notice that the twins had slumped back in their seats, covering their eyes with their hands and watching the movie through the gaps between their fingers, then closing their eyes completely to shut out the horrors of Doctor Kessler's laboratory.

The film reached its inevitable and bloody conclusion as the doctor was killed by his army of reanimated corpses and was himself turned into a reanimated corpse. The curtains closed and the lights were raised in the auditorium, sending a wave of cockroaches scuttling for cover.

Aunt Gisela and the twins said goodnight to Morbide, who left the cinema with Mrs Moritz for beetroot schnapps at the café on the corner of the street.

'Wasn't like that in my day,' grumbled Aunt Gisela, shaking her head, as she walked home with the twins. 'The movies used to be so blood-chilling that they got right into the marrow of your bones. And they didn't need electric shocks to do it.'

Greta and Feliks, who were too terrified to walk the

shadowy pavements of Death's Doorstep, took Aunt Gisela by the hand and led her down the middle of the deserted cobbled streets. Pale moonbeams illuminated the way forward, towards home. Feliks's face was milk-white with fear and Greta's mouth was so dry she found it almost impossible to speak without clacking like a raven.

'I thought you had more stomach,' said Aunt Gisela.

'Can't we go more quickly?' said Feliks. 'We don't know what's lurking ahead of us in the darkness.'

'It's not what's up ahead we need to worry about,' said Aunt Gisela deliciously, 'it's what's following on behind.'

Greta quickened her pace and Feliks gripped Aunt Gisela's hand so tightly that his fingernails sank deep into her skin.

The twins had still not shaken their fear at breakfast the next morning. Greta was so pale that her freckles stood out like measles.

'Rye-bread toast and cocoa will sort you both out,' said Aunt Gisela.

But Feliks only stared at her with tired and mournful eyes. He had slept fitfully, dreaming that his room was full of reanimated corpses. 'I'm not hungry,' he murmured, turning grimly to the obituaries on the last page of *The Informant.*

'What if we're murdered and reanimated one day?' asked Greta.

'If you spend all your time worrying about what's going to happen tomorrow, you'll never get anything done today,' said Aunt Gisela. She frowned at the twins. 'This is no good,' she groaned, watering a large green fern with the pot of cocoa and pushing the uneaten slices of rye bread through the bars of Karloff's cage. 'There's only one way to prove that there's no such thing as blood-sucking vampires and reanimated corpses. Get dressed and be quick about it.'

<hr/>

Aunt Gisela hurried with the twins to the tram stop on the corner of Donmerplatz.

'No, not that one,' said Aunt Gisela, as a tram rattled to a halt in front of them. 'We want the next one.'

'Where are we going now?' asked Greta.

'The Von Merhart movie studios, that's where,' said Aunt Gisela as another tram loomed into view. 'That's the tram for us.' She climbed on, dragging the twins behind her.

'Private tram,' said the conductor, holding up his hand as if to push Aunt Gisela and the twins back out into the street. 'Not for you and your sort.' He suddenly stopped and gasped. 'It's you!'

'Yes, it's me,' growled Aunt Gisela.

'I thought you were dead,' said the man.

Aunt Gisela poked him hard in the stomach with the tip of her umbrella.

'See?' she cackled. 'I'm not.'

Aunt Gisela paid for their tickets and sat with the twins, hugging them close to her to keep out the cold. It seemed strange to Feliks and Greta that so many people expected Aunt Gisela to be dead. Feliks half-wondered if she was a reanimated corpse herself.

The tram was empty, except for a tiny man with a bowler hat, who was engrossed in a novel entitled *Thirteen Deaths at Midnight*. The tram rattled across the Princess Euphenia Bridge, and into the Industrial District of the great city.

'Von Merhart Movie Studios,' cried the conductor as

the tram came to a shuddering halt, almost spilling the man with the bowler hat onto the floor.

'That's us,' said Aunt Gisela, and she stepped from the tram, followed by the twins. Their fellow passenger tipped his hat and saluted, scuttling off ahead of them.

The entrance to the studios was flanked by two hooded figures of carved black granite; one held a scythe in his skeletal hands, the other a noose. Feliks pulled back.

'Will there be reanimated corpses?' he whispered.

'Sure to be,' said Aunt Gisela briskly. 'Now keep up.' She hurried on towards a small wooden booth, where a young man stood reading a copy of *Fright Fortnightly*.

'Name?' said the man, without raising his eyes from the magazine.

'Gisela,' said Aunt Gisela. 'You're too young to know who I am, I expect?'

The man looked up in disbelief. 'Of course I know who you are,' he said, fumbling to open the gates.

'Where's that rogue Von Merhart filming today?' demanded Aunt Gisela.

'Sound Stage One,' said the young man.

'Then that's where we're going,' said Aunt Gisela, steaming ahead without a backwards glance, the twins struggling to keep up.

The young man called after them as a bell rang from deep inside the movie studios. 'Can I get your autograph?'

'No time,' cried Aunt Gisela. 'There's matters to be seen to and things to be put to rights.'

Without slowing, Aunt Gisela hurried on with the twins, passing a long-ago-discarded model of a vampire castle, rotting turrets made of wood and canvas and cardboard coffins that had turned to paste in the rain.

Finally coming to a halt outside the vast building that housed Sound Stage One, Aunt Gisela turned to face the twins.

'Real life is always more terrifying than the movies,' she said, pushing open the enormous door and leading the twins into the darkness. 'Now let's go and meet the evil Doctor Kessler.'

CHAPTER FOUR

———◆━◆◆◆━◆———

'**B**e careful,' whispered Feliks, as Greta stood on his foot.

'I can't see where I'm going,' said Greta.

'We should have brought torches,' muttered Aunt Gisela, stumbling in the gloom of the vast studio.

'Gisela?' said a voice, and Morbide appeared from the shadows. 'And the twins. This is a surprise.'

'They want to meet Doctor Kessler,' said Aunt Gisela, fishing a cigar from her pocket. 'At least, I think it will put things to rights when they do.'

'Kessler is here,' said Morbide with a sly grin. 'You're just in time to eat.' He turned and called out. 'A light, please.'

From high above an electric lantern glowed, casting a pool of light on the assembled party. Morbide took Greta by the hand, and together they walked to a small table.

'It is time you met our monsters,' said Morbide as a group of actors appeared from their dressing rooms and crowded round the visitors. Greta and Feliks took a step backwards, as two young men with raven-black hair wheeled a tea trolley into the studio.

'Greta, Feliks,' said Morbide. 'Permit me to introduce the brothers Vladek and Gabor.' Vladek and Gabor made low bows to the twins. 'The brothers play the most diabolical characters you could ever imagine.' A man in a bloodstained apron approached the table. 'And this is the Blind Butcher.'

There was a pot of strong black tea on the trolley and a plate of iced gingerbread. The twins sat at the table and Gabor poured the tea.

'There's someone missing from the picture,' said Morbide. 'Where is Doctor Kessler? Ah, there he is.'

The twins turned awkwardly, and there behind them stood Doctor Kessler. The reanimator of a thousand corpses.

'We have company,' said the Doctor, helping himself to a piece of gingerbread. 'How delightful.'

'You don't sound like Doctor Kessler,' ventured Feliks.

'The films are silent,' said Doctor Kessler. 'You have to imagine my voice.'

'We did,' said Greta. 'And it didn't sound like you.'

'I've never seen a woman die so well as our dear Gisela,'

murmured Doctor Kessler in admiration. 'We are honoured by your presence. You were the most beautiful, beautiful corpse.'

Aunt Gisela slapped the man gently on the shoulder. 'The things you say,' she crowed.

A tall and beautiful woman, with skin as pale as porcelain, slowly approached the table. She wore a long dress of white damask silk.

'China Doll,' said Morbide, rising to hold out a chair for the woman. His eyes seemed to sparkle. 'My love. My one true love.'

China Doll lowered her pale blue eyes, as a flush of blood brought colour to her cheeks.

'May I introduce the Mortenberg twins?' said Morbide. 'My very good friends.'

China Doll shook hands with the twins and smiled. Her fingers were so thin and pale they were almost translucent.

'Why do they call you China Doll?' Greta dared ask.

'My face,' whispered China Doll. 'My skin.'

'As pale as a corpse,' said Morbide with pride in his voice.

A squat man with no neck hurried out from a dressing

room, wiping make-up from his face.

'And that's Bullfrog,' said Morbide, as the man grinned widely and belched like a bullfrog. 'So called for obvious reasons.' The twins ate their gingerbread and talked happily with the actors, forgetting in an instant that they had ever been terrified of the movies.

◆━◆

After tea, Morbide took the twins and Aunt Gisela through to the make-up and wardrobe room.

Shelves ran along the back wall, stacked high with tins of greasepaint in numerous colours. There were wigs on wig blocks, a rack of fat suits and a shelf of assorted claws and false teeth.

The twins watched in fascination as a make-up artist covered Morbide's face with a thin layer of grey liquid greasepaint, to give him a lifeless look. The foundation was then dried under the metal dome of a hair dryer.

Morbide opened his mouth wide as a set of hideously deformed teeth were fitted into position. He stood in front of an electric fan to cool himself, as another man used putty to elongate Morbide's fingertips. Finally, Morbide lifted his wig from the block and placed it carefully on his head.

'Follow me,' said Morbide, leading the visitors out into the studio again.

There was more light than before, illuminating a row of houses that had been built from wood and plaster.

A bell rang and an unseen voice cried out, 'Silence in the studio.' With an ominous growl, two sleek, black guard dogs bounded across the floor.

'It's Von Merhart,' whispered Aunt Gisela to the twins, as a small man with a peaked cap and leather riding boots strode into the studio. 'I know him of old.'

Greta fidgeted in the harsh glare of the movie lights.

'*The Wheels That Turned*,' shouted a young man with a clapperboard. 'Scene forty-seven. Take five.'

Aunt Gisela and the twins stood silently as the lights were raised on a section of tramline that ran along the grim and forbidding street. China Doll lay on the rails as Morbide tied her securely in place with a long length of rope.

Feliks watched as a man turned the handle of the movie camera. Fritz Von Merhart sat back in his chair and barked through a megaphone of bright, polished brass. 'More blood!' There was no answer. 'Are you deaf?' he screamed.

'I said more blood!'

Greta shivered with excitement as a man hurried from behind the scenery with a bucket of blood, which he duly splashed over the tramlines, covering China Doll's beautiful white dress.

'Scene forty-seven!' cried the young man with the clapperboard as he sprang in front of the camera again. 'Take six.'

'And action!' screamed Von Merhart.

'He's famed for his ingenuity, demons rot him,' whispered Aunt Gisela to the twins. 'He's the first man ever to guillotine fifty people in a single movie.'

It was clear that Von Merhart had also devised a particularly cruel and unexpected death for the unfortunate China Doll.

A fog machine pumped out a constant vapour, which clung low around the set. As the camera rolled, China Doll kicked her feet and screamed so loudly that Feliks feared her lungs would burst. But they did not.

'What's wrong with you?' shrieked Von Merhart through his megaphone. 'You call that screaming? You think we have all day to waste?' He waved his hand towards the guard dogs. 'Perhaps Brute and Caligari can encourage you to scream more convincingly.'

'I don't like Von Merhart,' whispered Feliks.

'He looks evil to the core,' agreed Greta. 'You can see it in his eyes. Pure evil.'

'Who is that?' shouted Von Merhart. 'Who's there?' He swung round in his chair, glaring at the actors who had gathered behind him.

'Well?' he demanded. 'Speak up.'

Aunt Gisela stepped out from the shadows into the full glare of the studio lights. 'It's me,' she gurgled. 'Now what are you going to do about it?'

Von Merhart climbed out of his chair and slowly stalked towards Aunt Gisela, eyeing her narrowly as a dog observes a rabbit. A gold watch chain hung from his waistcoat pocket, with a golden fob shaped like a corpse dangling from a noose.

'You've grown old,' said Von Merhart at last.

'And you've grown ugly,' snarled Aunt Gisela.

'What are you doing here?' demanded the director. 'Come to plead for a job, have you?'

Aunt Gisela growled. 'I'd be dead in my grave before I

ever took another job from a weasel like you.'

'Best place for you,' snapped Von Merhart.

Greta had grown embarrassed by the argument and had drifted off towards a corner of the studio. A large set of plans were unrolled on a table, weighted in place by a dismembered foot of cast wax and the blade of a guillotine. Feliks joined his sister as Aunt Gisela and Von Merhart continued to bicker.

'It's a village,' said Greta, pointing at the plans. 'Is it a design for a movie set?'

Feliks shrugged. The designs were painstakingly drawn, with thatched houses and a cobbled market square.

'He doesn't like strangers looking,' whispered Bullfrog, appearing suddenly behind the twins. 'It's Von Merhart's labour of love, that is.'

Brute and Caligari, who had been sleeping beside the director's chair, whined uneasily, their ears pricked. They turned to the twins and uttered a throaty growl of warning.

'What are you doing?' screamed Von Merhart, running towards the twins with the dogs at his heels. 'Get away from there!' He snatched up the plans and rolled them tightly.

'And you,' he said, turning on Bullfrog. 'What do you

mean showing these roaches that which does not concern them?'

'He wasn't showing us anything,' protested Greta. 'He was telling us not to look.'

But it was no use. Von Merhart struck Bullfrog with the back of his hand and sent the actor scuttling back into the shadows.

'You leave him alone,' shouted Aunt Gisela.

'I'll do what I like,' spat Von Merhart. 'These are my studios.' The dogs barked fiercely, straining at the leash. 'Now get out of here. Brute and Caligari want blood and I'm inclined to let them have it.'

Feliks and Greta backed away, fearful that they would be consumed whole by the slavering hounds.

'Please can we go now?' whispered Feliks.

But Aunt Gisela would not be rushed. She slowly walked over to pick up her umbrella and bag.

'And now we can go,' she said to the twins. 'The smell around here is curdling my insides. You're the smell,' she added, glaring at Von Merhart. 'In case you're fool enough to be thinking otherwise.'

CHAPTER FIVE

'I thought Von Merhart was going to drop down dead in front of us,' said Morbide the next morning as he walked with Aunt Gisela and the twins across the Princess Euphenia Bridge towards the New Town. 'He was beetroot purple. The only other man I've ever known to turn that colour was not long for this world.'

'Would have served him right if he had bawled himself to death,' said Aunt Gisela, biting the end off a cigar and spitting it over the side of the bridge. 'No one would have mourned him in the whole of the great city.'

'No one would have mourned him!' cawed Karloff, soaring high above them, a bright flash of red against the pale grey sky.

'Quiet, bird,' chided Aunt Gisela. 'Or I'll take you back home and shut you up in your cage again.'

'He needs the exercise,' said Feliks. 'He's getting fat, poor old Karloff.'

'So why do you act in Von Merhart's movies?' Greta asked Morbide. 'If he treats you all so badly, can't you work for another director instead?'

'Von Merhart's the only director there is,' said Aunt Gisela, lighting her cigar. 'In Schwartzgarten, at any rate. More's the pity.'

'And acting's in my blood,' said Morbide with a sad smile. 'Something would die in here if I gave it up,' he added, indicating his heart. 'I was put on this earth to scare the life out of people.'

As if to illustrate his point he slipped in his fangs and lifted up the tails of his coat like a cape to leer menacingly at a passing boy, who ran off across the bridge and hid behind a lamp post.

'You see?' said Morbide, taking out the fangs and dropping them back inside his coat pocket. 'You can't buy that. Not for all the imperial crowns in Schwartzgarten.'

They made their way across Edvardplatz, and along a narrow side street.

'This is it,' said Morbide, pointing up at a brightly painted shop sign: F. DUTTLINGER. THEATRICAL SUPPLIERS.

The window was full of costumes, wigs and tins of greasepaint. A sign read: PURVEYOR OF DUTTLINGER'S PATENTED ARTIFICIAL HAIR.

Morbide opened the door for them. A bell jangled startlingly from the depths of the shop and Karloff squawked in alarm, digging his claws into Feliks's shoulder.

'Morbide!' cried a man, appearing from the back room. He wore a high starched collar, a drooping moustache and a bright orange wig, which had been combed into a severe side parting. His wrinkled face was thick with pallid make-up and his eyebrows had been drawn on with a stick of greasepaint.

'That's Duttlinger,' explained Morbide.

'And friends!' exclaimed the man, wincing as he ripped the moustache from his upper lip. 'You've brought friends!' He removed the wig to reveal a perfectly smooth head and wiped his face in a grubby towel. 'I've been practising, you see,' he explained to the twins. 'Always looking for an opportunity to dress up.' His face clean, he picked up a pair of spectacles from behind the counter and held them to his eyes. He stared hard at Aunt Gisela. 'Gisela, is that really you?

'Of course it's really me,' snapped Aunt Gisela.

'This is an honour,' said Duttlinger with a bow. 'A most distinct honour. You'll stay for tea? Of course you will;

there's always time for tea.' Without waiting for an answer, he led Morbide, Aunt Gisela and the twins into the back room, where a kettle sang noisily on the stove. Karloff took wing, whistling in reply to the steaming kettle. 'I might have something for you, Morbide,' said Duttlinger.

'The back brace?' asked Morbide, his voice trembling with excitement. 'Is it ready?'

'Perhaps,' said Duttlinger, smiling mischievously. He swung the kettle from the stove and poured five cups of peppermint tea. 'Perhaps.'

Aunt Gisela sat and Karloff swooped down to perch on the arm of her chair. Duttlinger gave the parrot a slice of stale gingerbread and made his way to the back of the room, where a cloth had been draped over a large and bulky object. He pulled back the cloth to reveal an enormous metal back brace.

'Is there something wrong with your back?' asked Feliks as he sipped the hot, sweet tea.

'No,' said Morbide, frowning and shaking his head.

Aunt Gisela cackled and lit a cigar, stroking Karloff's feathers as the parrot pecked away at the gingerbread.

'And that's the problem,' observed Duttlinger. 'There's

nothing wrong with his back whatsoever. This back brace will solve all that. You will be twisted and disfigured beyond your wildest imaginings, Morbide.'

Duttlinger assisted Morbide as he climbed into the enormous metal contraption.

'Is it comfortable?' asked Duttlinger, mounting a chair to tighten the upper screws of the brace.

'No,' replied Morbide, gritting his teeth. 'It isn't.'

'Excellent, excellent!' Duttlinger beamed. 'Then it must be working. The boots are a modification. Magnetic soles. You could climb a wall, if it was made of metal.'

Morbide lifted his leg and immediately his foot flung out and attached magnetically to a metal pipe in the corner of the room.

'What's wrong with it?' asked Morbide.

'Teething problems, I assure you,' said Duttlinger, attempting to prise Morbide's foot from the pipe. 'Perhaps I have too many magnets inside the boot. Yes, that would explain it.'

Once the back brace was firmly screwed into place, Morbide used thin wire to pull his nose out of shape, securing and concealing the wire on the top of his head beneath a wig of straggly black hair. He added bags beneath his eyes with a stick of purple greasepaint, and glued on a thick black moustache and eyebrows.

'Duttlinger's Patented Artificial Hair,' remarked Duttlinger, wheeling through a full-length mirror from the shop. 'The finest in the trade!'

Morbide stared at his reflection and twisted his smile until it contorted into the most terrifying grimace the twins had ever seen. The transformation was complete.

'Oh, that's very good,' said Aunt Gisela, tapping ash from her cigar. 'Very good indeed.'

'Very good indeed!' squawked Karloff, pecking up the last crumbs of gingerbread.

'And now,' said Morbide, 'it's time to transform the twins.'

'What do you mean?' asked Greta.

Morbide smiled, though the back brace was torture.

'Well, do you want fangs, or don't you?' said Aunt Gisela, rolling her eyes.

As Morbide practised walking in the back brace and Aunt Gisela sat sipping her tea, Duttlinger took the twins out into the shop and pointed to a chart displaying every style and size of artificial teeth imaginable. Greta gasped with excitement.

'What sort of teeth would you like?' asked Duttlinger.

'I want fangs like Morbide's,' replied Feliks.

'An excellent answer,' said Duttlinger, motioning to a large dentist's chair in the corner of the shop. 'Now, sit down, please.'

Feliks sat, opening his mouth wide as Duttlinger filled a mould with putty.

'Now bite,' said Duttlinger.

Feliks bit hard and his teeth sank deep into the putty. He could feel the mixture oozing around his gums. Duttlinger waited for the putty to harden, before reaching into the boy's mouth to remove the mould. Feliks clutched the arms of the chair tightly – it felt as though his teeth were being wrenched out.

'And now the little girl's turn,' said Duttlinger. 'Would you like receding gums with your fangs, perhaps? I think they might suit you.'

'Yes please,' said Greta, jumping up into the chair.

'Open wide, then,' said Duttlinger.

Chapter Six

Freed at last from the back brace, Morbide took Aunt Gisela and the twins for cocoa on Edvardplatz while Duttlinger set to work crafting the fangs in the back room of his shop. Karloff flapped high above them before swooping low over the canvas market stalls and pecking up scraps of food that had fallen between the cobbles.

'All he ever does is eat, that bird,' said Aunt Gisela. 'His stomach must think his throat's been cut.'

The twins and Aunt Gisela sat with Morbide outside the Myops's pastry shop on the corner of Edvardplatz, sipping their cocoa. It was almost noon and Morbide opened his pocket watch and counted down the seconds. As the sonorous boom of the Schwartzgarten clock sounded the hour, two wooden doors swung open behind the tower parapet and a pair of figures appeared from inside: the grinning figure of Death, and the headless figure of Life.

The figure of Life had not always been headless; many years before she had been possessed of a beautiful metal head, with an enchanting smile painted on her cold metal lips. But the large scythe which the figure of Death clutched in his hand was so sharp, and the mechanism was kept so well-oiled by the clock keeper, that one morning thirty years before, as the citizens of Schwartzgarten gathered on Edvardplatz in front of the clock tower, they had watched in horror as Death advanced on Life and, with an awful screech of metal, neatly severed her head from her neck, sending it plummeting down onto the cobbled square, crushing to death the President of the Guild of Master Locksmiths, who was unfortunate enough to be standing directly below. As a mark of respect to the President, the head had never been replaced.

After their cocoa, Morbide and Aunt Gisela took the twins to the Schwartzgarten Museum and the party spent an enjoyable afternoon staring at the wax sculptures of notable figures from Schwartzgarten's history. There were figures of the city's rulers, military leaders, writers, composers and other celebrated personages. But more interestingly, in a dark corner of one of the galleries, an area was set aside housing a grisly collection of waxworks and curiosities. There were shell fragments from the bombs of anarchists and wax figures of all the assassinated governors of the city. Karloff perched on the shoulder of Governor Orloff and pecked at his brittle wax ear, which crumbled to dust and sent the bird squawking in alarm.

Most fascinating of all to the twins was the painted metal head of the figure of Life, which had been unceremoniously decapitated on the clock tower so many years before. The head was badly battered, though not, of course, as badly battered as the head of the unlucky President of the Guild of Master Locksmiths. The scene had been grimly illustrated by a faded sepia photograph, hand-tinted in red to give an impression of the quantity of blood spilt that unfortunate morning.

As they slowly made their way back to Duttlinger's, Feliks asked if they might visit the Schwartzgarten Imperial Bookshop on the way. It was an intimidating shop, with buttressed walls of grey sandstone. High above, carved gargoyles leered out over the crowded streets, their wings outstretched and teeth bared.

'Gives me the shivers,' said Aunt Gisela, as she bustled inside behind Morbide and the twins. 'And that's saying something.'

Karloff perched quietly on Feliks's shoulder, nibbling gently at the boy's ear.

It was an enormous repository, aching under the weight of books, with dizzying mahogany ladders reaching up to the highest and dustiest shelves.

'I don't like this place. Not at all, I don't,' muttered Aunt Gisela, shuddering as an icy draught seemed to clutch at her spine. 'More like a great tomb for the dead than a place for the living.'

Leaving Feliks with Aunt Gisela and Morbide in the cookery section of the bookshop, Greta set off to explore. Wandering idly among the shelves, she stumbled upon a dark corner where the bookshelves were tightly grouped together under a sign marked: MURDER, MAYHEM AND THE MACABRE.

She reached up and pulled out a large book with a crimson dust jacket, printed in gold with the words *A Directory of Dark Happenings*. The book was an illustrated dictionary of all the dark, evil and murderous events that had taken place in the city of Schwartzgarten, and ran to many hundreds of pages. Certain that Fate had guided her hand, Greta smiled and made her way to the counter to pay.

'Five imperial crowns,' said the bookseller as Greta carefully placed the directory before him. 'But don't you think this book will give you nightmares?'

'I hope it will,' replied Greta earnestly, who felt fearless since she had discovered that there was no such thing as a reanimated corpse. She reached deep into her pockets and dredged up handfuls of curselings, which she heaped in a pile on the counter.

'We'll be here until the end of time,' grumbled a large woman standing in the queue, as Greta began to count out her coins. The woman wore an ugly hat of crushed black velvet, adorned with ostrich feathers. She carried in her arms a stack of adventure books for her daughter, who stood beside her wearing an even uglier hat of scarlet velvet and emu feathers.

'She is poor, Mother,' said the girl, clicking her tongue impatiently. 'She probably doesn't even have enough money to buy the book.'

'Quite right, my precious one,' agreed the girl's mother. 'She probably doesn't.' She swept Greta to one side with a powerful arm and tapped her umbrella violently on the counter.

'I am rich and I am busy,' she barked at the bookseller. 'I do not have time to wait for gutter rats who cannot afford to pay.'

'Gutter rats,' smirked the daughter.

The woman dropped the enormous heap of books on the counter in front of the bookseller and his face disappeared entirely from view.

It took Greta some moments to collect her thoughts, staring open-mouthed at the disagreeable and ugly-hatted woman. But when Greta did finally manage to speak, the words belched out of her in uncomfortable hiccups of fury.

'I am not a gutter rat,' she said. 'I am Greta Mortenberg.'

'You think I care who you are?' replied the woman. 'Gutter rat or not.'

Greta stood her ground. 'I do have enough money,' she continued. 'Because I've been saving it up in one of Aunt Gisela's empty cigar boxes.'

'I do not have time to wait,' insisted the woman, lifting the top book from the pile to reveal the bookseller's nose, which she prodded with the tip of her umbrella.

'Do please desist, madam,' uttered the man, holding

up his hands as if attempting to protect himself from an advancing bear.

'Do it again, Mother,' said the daughter, clapping her hands.

This was too much for Greta. She opened her mouth wide and screamed: 'I WAS HERE FIRST!'

Even the woman with the ugly hat was surprised by the ferocity of the outburst. On the other side of the shop, Feliks, Aunt Gisela and Morbide turned to see what had occured.

'The little girl is quite right,' said a voice from the crowd that had quickly gathered around the counter.

The ugly-hatted woman spun round furiously in the direction of the voice and flushed crimson from the neck up.

'WHAT?' demanded the woman. 'Who said that? Who spoke?'

'Me,' said the voice. 'I spoke.'

Greta turned as a tall, slim, elegant woman with purple lipstick and a bob of black hair stepped from the crowd. She wore a beautifully tailored dress of grey wolf's-tooth tweed with a collar of black mink, and buckled shoes that tapered at the back to form exquisite stiletto heels. A small black pillbox hat clung precariously to the side of her head, with a veil of black lace that swept just below her line of vision.

The woman with the ugly hat tottered backwards and uttered an explosive gurgle like the retch of a bilious raven.

'Olga Van Veenen,' stammered the daughter, tugging at her mother's overcoat both for support and attention.

'That is quite correct,' said the woman from the crowd. 'I am Olga Van Veenen.'

The daughter reached up to the counter and seized a book from the bottom of the pile, which sent the topmost books cascading down onto the bookseller.

'*The Skull That Grinned*,' said the daughter. 'We've just bought your book.'

'But you haven't bought my book yet, have you?' said Olga firmly, tugging the book from the daughter's grip. 'Because your mother pushed in front of this little girl.'

'Gutter rat,' said the daughter, missing Olga's point entirely. 'Will you signature it for me?'

'The word is "autograph",' corrected Olga Van Veenen, opening the cover of the book and producing a diamond-encrusted fountain pen as if from mid-air. 'What is your name?'

'Bernadette Biddulph,' said the daughter.

'Not you,' said Olga, and turned to face Greta. 'You.'

'Greta Mortenberg,' whispered Greta.

Olga autographed the book with an elegant swirl of purple ink. She pressed the volume into Greta's hands.

'Darling child,' she purred. Then, turning to the bookseller, 'Please charge the book to my account. And add whatever book Greta Mortenberg had intended to buy before this rhino forced her way to the counter.'

The woman with the ugly hat gaped.

'Please close your mouth,' said Olga. 'I am about to dine.' She turned and swept through the crowd.

Greta opened *The Skull That Grinned* and gazed at the inscription. 'To Greta Mortenberg,' she read, 'with love from Olga Van Veenen.'

Beneath this Olga had drawn a cartoon of the woman with the ugly hat's ugly hat and beneath this she had written in capital letters: AN EXTREMELY UGLY HAT.

Greta giggled and closed the book carefully, so as not to smudge the fresh ink.

'Olga Van Veenen suffers from writer's block,' said Feliks as they sat in Duttlinger's shop, waiting to be fitted with their fangs. 'She hasn't published a new book in five years. I read an article in *The Informant*. It's very sad, I suppose. She said it was her secret sorrow, not to have put pen to paper in so long.'

Greta sat up suddenly as Duttlinger appeared from the back room, clutching a small box in either hand. 'At last,' he declared. 'The work is done. And not a moment too soon. Another tick of the clock and you might have been overcome with anticipation.' He approached the twins and held out the boxes, one marked G. Mortenberg and the other, F. Mortenberg.

Greta and Feliks opened the boxes and gazed approvingly at their new fangs.

'You may find them uncomfortable at first,' explained Duttlinger as the twins carefully slipped the teeth into place. 'But you will grow used to them in time.' He held up a mirror so the twins could admire their reflections. 'The finished effect is a desirable one, I think.'

Duttlinger was a master of his art and had modelled

the teeth to perfection. Feliks's fangs were as sharp as needles, and Greta's were made more terrifying still by the addition of inflamed and bloodied gums, which had been moulded from red India rubber. Handing an apple to Greta and Feliks, Duttlinger instructed them to sink their fangs deep into the skin of the fruit, revealing the tell-tale vampire incisions. Feliks grinned and Greta squealed with delight.

Morbide applauded and Aunt Gisela glowed with pride at her newly be-fanged niece and nephew.

—◆—

That night, Greta lay in bed, reading by torchlight with the blanket pulled over her head. Even the excitement of the vampire fangs could not match the heart-stopping exhilaration of *The Skull That Grinned* – a story of kidnap, mistaken identity and many, many murders. She read through the night, only finishing the adventure as the sun slowly clawed its way through the gloom of the Old Town.

Inside the back cover of the book, Greta discovered a slip of card, printed in elegant copperplate writing. She read the words with mounting anticipation.

Did you enjoy this adventure? Perhaps you would like to become a member of the Van Veenen Adventure Society? If so, please send your name and address in an envelope to:

Claudius Estridge

Office 117B

The Guild of Publishers and Printers

Alexis Street

Schwartzgarten.

CHAPTER SEVEN

Early the next morning, Greta climbed out of bed and stole silently downstairs to the kitchen, careful not to wake Karloff in his cage, and took a stamp and envelope from Aunt Gisela's bureau. She wrote her name and address on a piece of paper, and slipped it inside the envelope, which she neatly addressed to Claudius Estridge. She pulled on her overcoat and set out to post the precious communication.

Two days later, a letter arrived, addressed to Greta Mortenberg. Inside was a large, folded sheet of paper.

'What's that?' asked Feliks suspiciously, cleaning his fangs with a toothbrush. 'Nobody ever sends us letters.'

'You don't know everything, Feliks,' replied Greta with a grin. 'Maybe there are some things you're just not supposed to know about.'

'Have you bought me a present?' asked Feliks.

'No,' said Greta, and hid the letter safely inside her

pocket. It was unusual for Greta not to share a secret with her twin, but she was worried that Feliks would disapprove of the letter.

Greta waited until midnight when the house was silent and crept downstairs. The cover had been pulled over Karloff's cage and the bird snored and whistled peacefully, but rather than risk waking him from his sleep by turning on the lights, Greta lit a candle from the cupboard and carried it carefully to the kitchen table. She sat down and unfolded the treasured letter. Printed on the paper, headed with the crest of the Van Veenen Adventure Society, were ten questions, with spaces for Greta to reply. She answered each question in turn.

QUESTION ONE: WHAT IS IT ABOUT OLGA VAN VEENEN'S BOOKS THAT YOU ADORE?

The incredible adventures, answered Greta in her neatest handwriting. *I want to have adventures too, like the characters in Olga Van Veenen's books.*

QUESTION TWO: WHAT ARE THE NAMES OF YOUR PARENTS?

I am an orphan, wrote Greta. *I have no parents any more. I live with my Aunt Gisela.*

QUESTION THREE: DO YOU HAVE ANY BROTHERS OR SISTERS?

I have a brother called Feliks. He reads books about food, but not adventure books. We are twins.

QUESTION FOUR: WHAT IS YOUR FAVOURITE FOOD?

Pistachio nougat, wrote Greta without a moment's hesitation. *And Aunt Gisela's vanilla pudding.*

QUESTION FIVE: WHAT FOOD DO YOU HATE?

Almonds, wrote Greta carefully. *I am allergic and so is Feliks (my brother, I wrote about him in question three). If we eat even a single almond we might die (in horrible fits of agony).*

QUESTION SIX: WHAT IS YOUR FAVOURITE SMELL?

Oil of petunia. It is the perfume that Aunt Gisela wears.

QUESTION SEVEN: ARE YOU VERY BRAVE?

Yes, answered Greta. She stopped and stared hard at the word; it seemed to sit lazily on the page. She added the word *VERY*, and moved on to the next question.

QUESTION EIGHT: WHAT TERRIFIES YOU MOST?

Greta sat back in her chair to consider the question. She wanted to write, *Nothing terrifies me*. But of course this was not entirely true. *Spiders*, she wrote. She looked back at her answer to question seven. It did not seem very brave to admit that she was terrified of spiders. So she scratched out the word *Spiders* and beneath it she wrote *ENORMOUS SPIDERS*. To make her point clear, she drew a large inky scribble of a spider on the paper; its spindly legs bristled with hairs and dangled down over question nine.

QUESTION NINE: WHAT IS YOUR GREATEST WISH?

This was an easy question to answer. *I want to see Olga Van Veenen again.*

She felt suddenly guilty and bit her lip.

And I want Feliks and Aunt Gisela to live for ever and ever and ever.

She stopped and pondered this, then added, *BUT I REALLY, REALLY, REALLY WANT TO SEE OLGA VAN VEENEN AGAIN.*

It was still not quite right, so she concluded her answer with the word *Please*, which she underlined several times in red ink.

QUESTION TEN: THE BOY, THE WOLF AND THE GINGERBREAD.

This was a different question entirely, laid out on the page as a riddle. It was also the final question.

A ferryman stands on the banks of the River Schwartz.

Beside the man is a plump little boy and a ravenous wolf. Beside the wolf, a parcel of gingerbread rests on a rock. The river runs fast. The ferryman can only carry one item at a time in his boat. How does the ferryman transport the boy, the wolf and the gingerbread safely to the opposite bank of the river?

Greta got up from the table and poured herself a glass of lingonberry cordial. She stared out of the window absently at the moonlit street and thought things through carefully. If the ferryman took the plump boy first, would the wolf eat the gingerbread? Did wolves even like gingerbread? Would the wolf eat the ferryman? The riddle didn't mention whether he was plump or not. It seemed impossible to reach the solution. Greta closed her eyes and imagined that she too was standing on the banks of the River Schwartz. There was the plump boy in front of her, there was the wolf, and beside them on a stone was the parcel of gingerbread. But where was the ferryman? It was easy to imagine the boy, the wolf and the gingerbread, but no matter how hard she tried she could not conjure up an image of the ferryman with his boat.

'Because there is no ferryman,' said Greta with a smile. 'That's why I can't imagine him.'

Once more she put pen to paper: *The river runs too fast so there are no ferrymen on the River Schwartz.*

She blotted the ink carefully, folded the paper and slid it inside the envelope. As before, she addressed the envelope care of Claudius Estridge.

<hr />

A week later, a small package arrived. Greta tore open the wrapping. Inside was a jewelled brooch and a label which read: *Olga Van Veenen welcomes you. Always wear your diamond pin so you will be recognised at once by other members of the Society.*

The letters V and V were shaped like intertwined serpents, spelt out in glittering gemstones.

'They're diamonds!' said Greta.

Aunt Gisela gave a violent bark of a laugh. 'Diamonds!' she said. 'They're not diamonds, they're paste!'

Ignoring her aunt, Greta carefully lifted the pin from its box.

'You could stab your eye out with a dirty great thing like that,' said Aunt Gisela as Greta pierced the lapel of her overcoat with the pin and gazed approvingly at her reflection in the mirror.

In the bottom of the box was an invitation, edged with gold and written in purple ink.

Olga Van Veenen invites you to a reading of the first draft of her new book at the Schwartzgarten Zoological Gardens, next Thursday morning at eleven o'clock precisely.

———◆———

Greta's excitement as the day of the book reading approached was only slightly marred by the arrival of a second invitation, addressed: *To Feliks Mortenberg*.

'You don't even read Olga Van Veenen's books,' said Greta. 'I don't see why you've been invited to the reading as well. You only read recipe books.'

'I didn't get a diamond pin,' said Feliks.

'Good,' said Greta. 'It wouldn't have been fair if you had.'

As requested in the invitation, the twins arrived outside the gates of the Schwartzgarten Zoological Gardens at precisely eleven o'clock in the morning. Aunt Gisela had left Karloff at home and stood alone, waving Greta and Feliks off as they showed their tickets to a keeper and hurried inside.

The zoo housed a grim menagerie of animals. There was a moulting anteater and an underfed tiger that walked round in circles impatiently, staring hungrily at any visitors who passed his cage. From time to time a penguin would become lost and wander from its pool and into the cage, where the tiger would eat it greedily.

But it was not the anteater, or the tiger, or even the unfortunate penguins that captivated the imaginations of the twins. They hurried on without a second glance, past the reptile house with the boa constrictor and the geckoes, past the insect house with the black widow spider and the wingless Madagascan hissing cockroach. On and on they ventured, to the furthest corner of the zoo and a large grey building, cast in concrete to resemble the Carpathian Mountains. Above the entrance was a sign which read: *The Carpathian Bat*. It was the only exhibit in the zoo that was still thriving. The native Schwartzgarten bats had found a hole in the concrete shell of the building and had begun to breed with the Carpathian bats at such a rate that the building was black with the sharp-toothed and leather-winged creatures.

As Greta and Feliks entered, a keeper was preparing to feed the bats, removing the lid from a large box of moths. The twins watched as the moths flew around the concrete cave in disorientated circles trying desperately to escape, only to be snapped out of the air by the ravenous bats. A small group of children had already gathered inside the bat house, shivering from the cold but watching the unfolding moth carnage with undisguised enjoyment. The floor was soon showered with dust from the moths' delicate wings, which Feliks noted added further drama to the scene.

'I hate bats,' said a girl in ponytails standing close to Greta. 'But I hate moths even more.'

The lapel of the girl's coat glittered, and Greta saw at once that she too was wearing the pin of the Van Veenen Adventure Society.

'Good afternoon, loyal members of the Society,' came a voice.

The children turned and there at the entrance to the cave-like chamber stood Olga Van Veenen. She seemed even taller than Greta remembered, dressed in an elegant skirt and jacket of Brammerhaus tweed, with a fox fur draped lifelessly over her shoulders.

'You are all very welcome,' Olga continued, taking the hand of the nearest child and patting it affectionately.

'Are you going to read to us from your new book?' asked the ponytailed girl, forcing her way forward to stand in front of Greta.

Olga smiled. 'All in good time,' she assured the girl. 'All in good time.'

The calm was suddenly cracked by a terrified shriek as a zookeeper stumbled into the bat house.

'The gate is open!' he screamed. 'The tiger's escaped!'

Olga glared at the man. 'Don't scream,' she commanded. 'You will terrify my friends.' She motioned to the members of the Van Veenen Adventure Society.

'And they'd be right to be terrified,' laughed the zookeeper, half-mad with terror. 'Have you seen the mess a beast like that leaves behind when he rips the head off a mortal being like you or me?'

'I have not,' replied Olga.

'It's enough to put a man off his goulash,' said the zookeeper grimly. 'I'll tell you that much.'

There came a bloodcurdling roar from outside the cave and the Carpathian bats, that had been roosting silently after satisfying their lust for moths, took wing around the chamber.

'It's in my hair!' screamed the ponytailed girl, as the claws of an unfortunate bat became entangled in her golden locks.

But there were more serious dangers for the assembled members of the Adventure Society. An orange and black muzzle appeared through the gloom.

'It's him,' rasped the zookeeper, backing against the wall. 'He's come for me!'

'Now keep calm, children,' said Olga firmly. 'He will do us no harm as long as we do nothing to enrage him.'

Feliks seized Greta tightly by the hand.

The tiger gave a low, guttural growl and snorted, a cloud of vapour forming in the icy bat house. This was too much for the zookeeper, who shrieked and fought his way madly through the swarming bats and fled out through the exit at the rear of the chamber.

The tiger slowly padded inside and gave another low growl, which filled the cave with the sickly stench of rotting meat. The effect on the Adventure Society was dramatic. There were screams and pleas for mercy; two boys collapsed in a dead faint and three of the more agile children climbed up the carved rock face to hang from the bat roost, safely out of harm's way.

The tiger swung his head and neatly batted the ponytailed girl against the concrete wall of the cavern, finally releasing the entangled Carpathian bat from her hair. It soared gratefully into the air only to be crunched up in the tiger's mighty jaws. The children who still had their wits about them followed the zookeeper's example and fled. Only Olga and the twins stood their ground, partly from defiance and partly from fear.

Greta whispered to Feliks. 'Help the other children,' she said. 'I'm going to distract the tiger.'

She waved her arms and poked out her tongue and the animal took a half-step back in surprise.

Unobserved, Feliks backed slowly away from the tiger. Silently, he shook the two boys who had fainted and helped them out of the cave. Greta meanwhile was leering at the tiger; she puffed up her cheeks and inserted a thumb in each nostril.

The tiger sat back on its haunches and Olga Van Veenen watched in spellbound silence.

Feliks returned on tiptoe, and motioned to the three children still hanging from the beam in the roof of the cave. He pointed to a vast pile of fetid bat droppings immediately below them, and watched as each child in turn dropped safely onto the pungent heap, before shepherding them out through the door.

'Now lock it,' whispered Greta, wrinkling up her nose and flapping her arms at the tiger, who was by turns baffled and fascinated.

Feliks did as his sister instructed and closed the door quietly, bolting it securely.

'What should we do now?' asked Olga, her eyes glittering in the darkness.

'Now we have to move to the other door,' whispered Greta. 'Very, very slowly.'

With their backs pressed against the wall of the circular chamber, Olga and the twins slowly made their way to the entrance. All the time Greta snorted at the tiger, pulled at her hair, poked out her tongue; anything to keep the creature distracted. But as soon as they reached the door

Greta shouted out,

'Now run!'

They slipped outside and the tiger sprang to his feet. He let out a roar and bounded towards the door; but he was too late. Greta, Feliks and Olga slammed the door shut behind them, and a group of zookeepers who had been cowering outside, preparing to sweep up the carnage, sprang to their aid; they chained and bolted the door as it quivered against the tiger's enormous weight.

'It's done,' said Greta with a grin.

Feliks grinned back. 'It's done.'

It was not until an hour later that it was considered safe enough to return the tiger to his cage, by which time he had consumed the greater part of the population of Carpathian bats and lay contentedly on the floor flicking his tail, surrounded by regurgitated wings and streaks of bat blood.

'There's no explaining it,' said the zookeeper, as the tiger was led away. 'He was chained in safe enough, I checked it myself.'

'You are asking me to believe that somebody deliberately released the tiger?' demanded the zoo director.

'That's exactly what I'm asking you to believe,' replied the zookeeper.

'Have you been drinking?' asked the zoo director.

'One or two sips of brandy to steady my nerves,' confessed the zookeeper. 'But no more than was strictly necessary.'

A reporter from *The Informant* took notes as Olga and the twins posed beside the tiger cage for the photographer.

'My darlings, you have saved my life,' said Olga. 'And for that I will be eternally in your debt.' She swung the fox fur over her shoulder and turned to the photographer. 'Without the bravery and ingenuity of Greta and Feliks Mortenberg, I would undoubtedly have perished.'

'Smile,' said the photographer, as the flashbulb exploded in a halo of blinding light.

CHAPTER EIGHT

Olga Van Veenen, who was much affected by the adventures of the morning, abandoned the reading of her new book. She took her leave of the twins, and Greta and Feliks spent a pleasant afternoon guiding the unfortunate penguins away from the tiger's cage.

As had been arranged, the twins walked to Edvardplatz to meet Aunt Gisela for hot cocoa at the Myops's pastry shop. She was examining the evening edition of *The Informant* as they approached the square. On the front page of the newspaper was a full-length photograph of Olga Van Veenen and the twins beside the tiger's cage.

'I just knew you had something heroic coursing through your veins,' said Aunt Gisela. 'Good blood, I say. I shouldn't be surprised if the Governor of Schwartzgarten himself gets to hear of this.'

As they walked home to the Old Town, browsing the antique bookstalls that lined the South Bank of the River Schwartz, they recounted the adventures of the afternoon. Feliks picked up an ancient leather-bound volume of recipes, *Foods Peculiar To These Parts*.

He turned the pages of the book.

Caramel Pastries, As Enjoyed At The Table Of Good Prince Eugene.

Feliks grinned and smacked his lips.

'You want the book, it's yours,' said Aunt Gisela, opening her bag and taking out a handful of curselings, which she thrust into the hands of the stallholder.

'The tiger's safely back in his cage, and nobody was mauled to death,' said Feliks cheerfully as they crossed the Princess Euphenia Bridge into the Old Town. 'And I've got my book. I suppose that's a happy ending, isn't it?'

'But life never ends happily,' sighed Greta.

Black clouds bled across the evening sky like ink in water, accompanied by the crack and boom of thunder overhead. There was a steady spattering of rain and ribbons of lightning sparked above the rooftops.

'It's lazy rain,' said Aunt Gisela. 'It goes right through you. Nothing to fret over.'

Feliks hugged the recipe book tightly to his chest,

protected beneath his overcoat, and followed his aunt and sister along the narrow streets of the Old Town.

'What's this, then?' said Aunt Gisela as they arrived home. She picked up a box that had been placed outside the front door, tied with scarlet ribbon. The aroma was unmistakable. 'Almonds,' she purred, her nostrils quivering as she unlocked the door and hurried the twins inside to the warmth of the kitchen.

'There's a label,' said Greta. 'To Feliks and Greta. In honour of your bravery.'

Aunt Gisela untied the ribbon and lifted the cake from the box. 'Almond marzipan cake!' she croaked. 'Just look at that!'

Feliks's heart sank.

'It's the fundamental good in people,' said Aunt Gisela, slipping off her overcoat and cutting a thick wedge of the marzipan cake. She licked her fingers. 'You do something heroic and the good citizens of the city, they're falling over themselves to reward you both.'

'But we don't like almonds,' groaned Feliks.

'You know that and I know that,' said Aunt Gisela, taking out a plate of cinnamon buns and a jug of cold milk from the icebox, which she set down on the table for the twins. 'Who else knows it?'

'Doctor Lempick does,' said Greta.

'Why would Doctor Lempick want to poison you with almonds?' said Aunt Gisela. 'He knows you're allergic.'

'You haven't paid him for your heart tonic,' said Feliks.

Aunt Gisela laughed. 'And you think he goes about the streets of Schwartzgarten,' she said, 'poisoning the patients that haven't paid their bills? He wouldn't have a patient living in the whole city!' She held her copy of *The Informant* to the wall above the stove. 'I'll have it framed,' she said proudly. 'My two heroes.'

'And Olga Van Veenen,' added Greta. 'She was a hero too.'

Feliks idly dipped a piece of cinnamon bun into his glass of milk. He watched Aunt Gisela enviously as she took a large mouthful of the almond marzipan cake.

'Good cake,' muttered Aunt Gisela, sending a shower of crumbs and currants cascading down onto the floor.

'Did you see the newspaper?' Greta asked Morbide as he returned home from the movie studios.

'Have some cake,' said Aunt Gisela, cutting an

enormous slice and heaping it onto a plate.

Morbide shook his head. 'I don't have an appetite for marzipan.'

'Each to his own,' said Aunt Gisela. 'The bird'll have it.'

But Karloff turned his beak and pecked instead at his cuttlefish.

'*Twins Capture Tiger*,' said Greta, reading from the newspaper. '*Twins Greta and Feliks Mortenberg—*'

'Only it doesn't say "Greta",' interrupted Feliks. 'It says Gretel.'

Aunt Gisela gave a hollow cough and Greta looked up from the newspaper.

'That doesn't feel so good,' said Aunt Gisela, reaching across to the cupboard. She poured a glass of apple brandy and eased herself into a chair.

'Is something the matter?' asked Morbide.

'Nothing a sip of brandy won't put right,' said Aunt Gisela, draining the glass. 'Indigestion water. Soothes my gut.'

Karloff stretched and flapped his wings.

'Soothes my gut! Soothes my gut!' he squawked.

The twins knew all too well that Aunt Gisela was not a healthy woman. She smoked too many cigars, she ate too much rich food and drank too many glasses of apple brandy. Doctor Lempick had told her repeatedly that cigars and brandy were bad for her health, but Aunt Gisela had taken no notice. 'What's good for the soul, is good for the liver,' she had always said.

Feliks was relieved to see Aunt Gisela pull herself to her feet and pour another glass of brandy. 'My twins, my brave little heroes. I'll remember this afternoon till the end of my days!'

But then her eyelids flickered and she stumbled against the table, falling backwards onto the floor and dragging the tablecloth with her. The bottle of apple brandy smashed on the tiles, and the almond marzipan cake rolled across the rug, wobbling to a standstill beside Aunt Gisela's motionless face.

Morbide jumped up from his chair. 'Gisela?' he whispered, his face paler than ever and his eyes dark with dread. He leant over Aunt Gisela and listened hard for signs of life. But there was nothing to be heard except the gentle rattle of air escaping her lungs as she gasped her final breath.

'Quickly!' cried Morbide. 'Call for help!'

Greta ran to the hall and telephoned for the doctor. But of course it was too late for that. When Doctor Lempick arrived the body was already cooling.

'She's dead,' said the doctor.

'But she can't be,' protested Greta.

'Her heart gave out,' said Doctor Lempick. 'Too much brandy, too many cigars. I was forever warning her, but did she listen? No, she did not. Well, let this be a lesson to her.'

'What do we do now?' asked Feliks.

'Now?' said Doctor Lempick. 'Now I shall telephone for Schroeder the Undertaker.'

———✦———

'So the old girl's dead, is she?' said Schroeder, having driven the short distance from his shop in his motor hearse.

'He reeks of beetroot schnapps,' whispered Greta to Feliks, as Schroeder and his son carried an empty coffin into the house.

'Out of the way, then,' said Schroeder, weaving into

the kitchen and steadying himself against the door frame. 'I've got to box the old buzzard and carry her out.'

Greta and Feliks waited with Morbide outside the kitchen door as the undertakers prepared to remove Aunt Gisela's body. Karloff clicked his tongue, pressing his beak gently against Feliks's neck.

At last the door opened, and the undertakers emerged with the coffin.

'Time to carry the old baggage away,' said Schroeder with a smirk.

Karloff screeched loudly, taking wing and scratching at Schroeder's face. The undertaker screamed and cursed as he and his son manoeuvred the coffin along the hall and out into the street.

'She's dead,' squawked Karloff. 'Dead and murdered! Dead and murdered!'

The undertakers heaved the coffin into the back of the waiting motor hearse.

'Wave goodbye,' said Schroeder, grinning at the twins as he slammed the door shut.

Morbide uttered a curse under his breath and spat into the gutter.

The twins stood on the pavement outside the house, frozen with shock. Their dear, beloved Aunt Gisela was dead and gone.

CHAPTER NINE

E arly the next morning, Morbide and the twins set off for Schroeder's shop, to pay their respects to Aunt Gisela. Life for Greta and Feliks had changed in an instant. They felt more alone in the world than they had ever imagined possible.

Schroeder smirked as he beckoned the party inside. A photograph of the man hung in a frame on the wall, dressed in the full regalia of the Guild of Undertakers.

'Old Gisela's husband, he was the same,' said Schroeder. 'Your uncle. Always drinking, always smoking. It's people like that who keep people like me in business.'

'We never knew him,' said Feliks. 'He died before we were born.'

'What sort of man was he?' asked Greta.

'Stocky,' replied Schroeder. 'Took eight men to carry him to his grave.'

He took them into a small room behind his office. There, on a silver stand, was Aunt Gisela's open coffin.

It was a beautiful casket of polished rosewood, lined with magenta silk.

'But we can't afford to pay,' said Feliks. 'Aunt Gisela didn't have enough money to pay for a rosewood coffin.'

'All taken care of,' said Schroeder. 'Anonymous benefactor. Otherwise I would have dropped her into her grave in a sack. Best place for an actor.'

'But who?' asked Greta, staring at the man in bewilderment. 'Who paid for her to be buried?'

'Don't you know what anonymous means?' said Schroeder. 'Buy yourself a dictionary and look it up.'

Greta was preparing to kick the man but Feliks held her back.

The twins peered into the coffin. Aunt Gisela's fingers were folded tidily in front of her; the position they often took when she slipped into a brandy-induced haze beside the kitchen stove. But her face had been robbed of all trace of life. The skin was yellow and wax-like, and her mouth was open wide, revealing her white and motionless tongue inside.

Greta shuddered and took a step backwards.

'I know,' said Schroeder. 'Enough to give you the

horrors, isn't it?'

Feliks wanted to reach in and kiss Aunt Gisela on the head, but somehow he could not summon the courage to do so.

'What's that smell?' said Schroeder, suddenly sniffing at the air above the coffin. He bent over Aunt Gisela's face then recoiled in horror.

'What is it?' asked Feliks, startled. 'What's wrong?

'Her breath,' whispered Schroeder. 'Smell her breath.'

Greta leant into the coffin and sniffed at Aunt Gisela's gaping mouth. There was a strong and unmistakable smell of beetroot schnapps.

'But...' began Greta, stepping back from the coffin. 'But that's impossible.'

'Maybe she's not really dead,' gasped Schroeder.

'What do you mean?' said Feliks quietly.

'I hardly dare utter it,' said Schroeder. He cast an eye over his shoulder.

'Go on,' said Greta.

Schroeder let out a hoarse whisper. 'Maybe your aunt rises from that coffin to swill her mouth with beetroot schnapps like she did when she was living.'

Feliks staggered backwards.

Schroeder held up a half-empty bottle of beetroot schnapps and an explosion of laughter escaped his lips.

'It was me,' he screamed, banging on the side of the coffin. 'It wasn't her. I poured it in! Of course the old woman's dead really!'

Greta's face flushed red with anger and Feliks grasped her hand, fearful that his sister would fly at the undertaker and make matters worse.

Schroeder backed up against another coffin, which stood on trestles behind him. He was laughing so hard he had to reach out a hand to steady himself on the coffin lid. As he did so, the lid began to creak open. Schroeder gave a strangulated cry as a figure sat up in the coffin: a figure with raven-black hair and razor-sharp fangs.

'Do you have to make so much noise?' inquired the figure politely. 'Some of us are trying to sleep.'

Schroeder collapsed in a dead faint and the twins stood grinning at the occupant of the coffin.

'He deserved it,' grumbled Morbide, removing the wig and fangs and pouring a generous splash of beetroot schnapps onto the head of the outstretched undertaker to bring him round.

—•—

'I wish we could reanimate corpses like Doctor Kessler,' said Greta, as they wandered home along the cobbles. Like bellows on a failing fire, talking seemed to keep the flickering memory of Aunt Gisela alive. 'We could reanimate Aunt Gisela and bring her back to us again.'

Feliks shivered. He did not find this a comforting thought.

That night he lay in bed, with the quilt pulled up over his head. He imagined the lifeless corpse of Aunt Gisela walking the streets from Schroeder's shop, pushing open the downstairs door and climbing the stairs. He imagined Aunt Gisela tucking him in and kissing him goodnight with her grey, dead lips.

—•—

Aunt Gisela was buried the following morning. The twins walked behind the hearse as it rattled over the cobbles towards the Schwartzgarten Municipal Cemetery. The monster actors had turned out in force, and many hundreds of movie fans lined the pathway that wound through the cemetery.

'I never knew that Aunt Gisela was so famous,' said Feliks.

The coffin appeared larger than the twins had remembered, as it was carried out of the hearse by four ancient-looking pallbearers, whose services had also been paid for by the anonymous admirer.

By the time they reached the graveside the pallbearers were almost crawling along on their hands and knees.

'It ages them,' said Schroeder's son. 'The weight of all those bodies.'

Slowly, the coffin was lowered into the grave and Schroeder smirked at a job well done.

It was a cold day and whatever moisture formed in the corners of Greta's eyes quickly froze. Feliks was too unhappy to cry.

'Dead and gone,' squawked Karloff as he circled above the grave. 'Dead and gone!'

The graveside had been piled deep with floral arrangements to commemorate the passing of the great

Gisela Mortenberg. On one of the larger floral tributes Aunt Gisela's name had been picked out in ivy and blood-red roses.

Greta reached across to pick up a card that had been tied with black ribbon to a bouquet of ivory lilies. There was a message, written in purple ink.

'With deep sadness at your loss.' As Greta read the dedication quietly under her breath, the words seemed to condense in the frosty morning air. 'From Olga Van Veenen.'

◆

Fritz Von Merhart, of course, was absent from the funeral party. He had risen early to send a telegram, and spent much of the day pacing the floor of his office, waiting for a response to the communication.

The sun sank low in the sky, but still no answer came. As night fell, Von Merhart lit the candelabrum on his desk and sat down to compose a letter.

It seems my telegram did little to stir you into action, he wrote. *Gisela Mortenberg is dead and your intentions seem clear to me. The price for my silence has increased…*

A creak from the shadows disturbed his concentration. He looked up from the desk.

A skeleton, which hung from a noose beside the door, swayed gently in the breeze, its bones rattling quietly. Von Merhart smiled. His office was full of mementoes; the walls were adorned with posters of his most successful horror movies, and a row of wax heads stood upon a shelf, their glass eyes sparkling demonically in the flickering candlelight. Outside, a crack of lightning lit the sky.

Von Merhart continued to write his letter.

...unless you agree to my terms, I shall at once inform the police...

Again, he was distracted by a noise. He rose from his desk, carrying the candelabrum with him as he walked to the door. He turned the handle and looked out across the deserted studio below, the flickering flames of the candles casting long shadows across the set of Doctor Kessler's laboratory.

'Who's here?' called Von Merhart, his voice echoing around the cavernous building. 'Caligari! Brute!' But there was no answer and he muttered angrily to himself. 'Lazy hounds.'

He returned to his office, and closed the door. A figure seemed to move in the shadows. Half-believing that it was a trick of the light, Von Merhart reached out to the electric switch on the wall. But it was useless; the power had been cut. There were footsteps behind him and Von Merhart turned sharply. 'Who are you?' he whispered. 'What are you doing here?' Lightning streaked across the sky. 'Show yourself!' he demanded.

There was a portentous roll of thunder and rain battered against the window. The intruder took a step forward.

'Is it you?' whispered Von Merhart, straining his eyes to make out the figure as it slowly advanced on him through the shadows.

'You've become greedy, Von Merhart,' said a voice. 'And the greedy must be punished.'

Von Merhart's throat constricted. 'Don't be foolish,' he stammered. 'Think how useful I can be to you.'

'Oh, but I have thought about it,' said the voice, 'and I've come to the unavoidable conclusion that you've outlived your usefulness.'

There was a flash of gold from a narrow stiletto blade

and Von Merhart cried out in the darkness.

'Help me,' he gasped.

The assailant turned and walked quickly from the room.

Von Merhart stumbled blindly, clutching at his bleeding throat. He staggered downstairs from his office and out through the doors of the studio. Gasoline had been ignited in the sound stages and flames were already engulfing the building.

Von Merhart gave a gurgling cry. He fell to his knees and toppled forward onto the cobbles. He was quite dead.

CHAPTER TEN

When Mrs Moritz was not playing piano at the Cinema of Blood, she told fortunes on Donmerplatz, in a small, dark shop that was overrun by cats. And it was back to the shop that Mrs Moritz had invited the twins after the funeral of Aunt Gisela.

Mrs Moritz smiled kindly, as the twins sipped from cups of strong, sweet coffee. 'You want your fortune told, that's what you want,' she said. 'That'll show you the path Fate's got mapped out for you.'

Feliks was not at all sure that that was what they wanted. What they wanted was Aunt Gisela, but no amount of fortune-telling was going to bring her back to them. So he gave a half-hearted smile and nodded his head. 'Thank you, Mrs Moritz.' He took a last sip of the coffee.

'Good,' said Mrs Moritz. 'Now swill round the cup and let the coffee grounds unlock their secrets.'

Feliks did as he was told. Mrs Moritz took the cup from him and tipped the grounds into a saucer.

'Is it dark in here, or am I going blind?' she asked.

'It is dark,' said Greta.

'All adds to the mystery,' said Mrs Moritz, but nevertheless turned up the gas lamp. She held the saucer close to her eyes.

'What can you see?' asked Greta.

'That shouldn't be there,' said Mrs Moritz, peering carefully at the saucer.

'Have you seen something bad?' whispered Feliks.

'Cat hair,' said Mrs Moritz, pulling a long orange strand from the coffee grounds. 'I swear by all that's mystical, that cat's moulting.'

'This is stupid,' said Greta.

'Don't talk ill of the coffee grounds,' said Mrs Moritz. 'Now let's see what Fate has in store for you both.' She gave a reassuring grunt and nodded. 'Not to worry,' she said at last, crossing her fingers under the table. 'It all ends happily for the pair of you.'

'You do know she doesn't really see anything?' said Greta, as she walked with her brother through the dark and deserted streets of the Old Town on their way home.

'I know,' said Feliks.

'Then why did you let her do it?'

'It makes her feel good,' said Feliks. 'And anyway, she said that things are going to get better. Even if it isn't true it's still nice to hear it.'

They rounded a corner and were about to cross the cobbles for home, when Greta suddenly pulled Feliks backwards.

'What is it?' he whispered.

Greta pointed across the street. There, in front of the house, stood a constable and the Inspector of Police. Morbide was at the open doorway, looming above the two men.

'Oh yes, I know you,' said the Inspector, fighting to retain his composure. 'I know your type.'

'What type is that?' growled Morbide.

'Monster on screen and off,' said the Inspector. 'It seems you had a motive for the murder of Fritz Von Merhart.'

'I hated the little cockroach, if that's what you mean,' replied Morbide.

This was too much for Greta, who ran across the street, followed by Feliks.

'Is Von Merhart really dead?' she demanded.

'With two puncture marks in his neck,' said the constable, deliciously. 'Like a monster done it.'

'But everybody hated Von Merhart,' cried Greta. 'Morbide's innocent.'

'That's for the courts to decide, isn't it?' said the Inspector.

'You can't take him,' said Feliks. 'He hasn't done anything wrong.'

'That's what you think,' giggled the constable, 'But Von Merhart scrawled Morbide's name in his very own blood.'

The twins watched in silence as Morbide was led down the steps and into the waiting police wagon. They waited until the wagon had passed from sight, then turned miserably towards the open door of the house.

'I don't know where you think you're going, my poppets,' said a voice.

The twins turned suddenly, to see a woman emerging from an alleyway. She was short and severe, with thick plaits of yellow hair coiled on either side of her unusually round head.

'Who are you?' demanded Feliks.

'Quiet,' barked the woman, breathing garlic fumes over the twins. 'I'm the Superintendent, so get that thought fixed in your skulls. I'm the one asking questions. You're the twins with the dead auntie all tucked up warm in her grave, are you?'

'We are the Mortenberg twins,' said Greta with dignity.

'Like I thought,' said the Superintendent, cracking her knuckles. 'I've come to take you to your new home.'

'Our new home?' said Feliks. 'But this is our home.'

'Not now it isn't,' said the Superintendent with a grin. 'It's up for auction to pay off debts.'

'What debts?' asked Greta.

'To pay for your board and lodging in the Schwartzgarten Reformatory for Maladjusted Children,' replied the Superintendent. 'That's what debts.'

'The Reformatory?' said Feliks, his mouth suddenly dry.

'But we're not maladjusted,' insisted Greta.

'Not yet.' The Superintendent smirked. 'A few days in the nut hole and I'll squeeze that spirit out of you, my poppets.'

'But what about our parrot?' asked Greta, as Karloff soared overhead.

'No place for parrots,' said the Superintendent, 'not unless it's to add body to the goulash!'

She yelled and clapped her hands and sent Karloff squawking off in alarm. She cracked her knuckles loudly again and marched the twins to a waiting motor van, which purred and spluttered at the end of the street.

————

'Welcome to your new home,' said the Superintendent, as the van rolled up outside the great wooden gates of the Schwartzgarten Reformatory for Maladjusted Children. She switched off the engine, and dragged the twins from inside the van.

'Open up!' she cried, beating her fist against the gates.

'Who is it?' called a voice.

'Who do you think it is?' said the Superintendent. 'Your old mother, come to kiss it all better?'

The doors were opened by an elderly gatekeeper, and the Superintendent pushed the twins inside, onto a cobbled courtyard. The Reformatory was housed inside a vast building that dwarfed the children as they stared up at its grim, grey walls. Faces peered out at them from behind barred windows, and the stench of fish goulash hung everywhere about the place.

The Superintendent led the twins across the courtyard and up a winding flight of steps.

'This way, and quickly,' she said, opening a door to a small office. She pulled back the shutters of a roll-top desk and took out a document that she laid on the table in front of the twins.

'And you're both orphans, you say?' she said, taking out a fountain pen and unscrewing the lid.

'Yes,' said Feliks. 'Our parents died in very tragic circumstances.'

'In a terrible motoring accident,' added Greta.

'My heart bleeds,' said the Superintendent. 'Now sign there and there and once more there.'

Feliks struggled to read the document in the half-light of the office.

'I didn't say read it, did I?' snapped the Superintendent. 'Just sign it.'

'It's important to read everything thoroughly before signing,' said Feliks.

'It's important to eat and keep your bellies full,' said the Superintendent. 'But you won't eat a scrap if you don't do as you're told. Now sign the paper.'

The twins signed the paper; Feliks first, and then Greta.

'Count yourselves lucky that you've got me to look after you now, my little poppets,' continued the Superintendent as she pushed the twins from the office and up a spiral staircase of iron steps, which wound through the very heart of the enormous building. 'I'll make your lives here a living nightmare. It'll take your minds off the fact that you're poor little orphans with no mother or father to make all the bad things go away.'

The Reformatory was constructed of vast iron beams, like the skeleton of a giant metal beast. A bewildering hum of noise gave it an eerie life; a strange warble that ebbed and flowed like the tide of an immense and mournful sea.

'It's voices,' whispered Greta, clutching hold of Feliks's arm. 'It's the sound of children's voices.'

'All my little poppets, that's what that is,' said the Superintendent, stopping on a step and peering down at the twins through the gloom. 'All my little angel poppets. It's like music to my soul, the eternal hum of it.' She leant hard against the handrail and screamed out into the darkness. 'Two more inmates to swell the numbers. Two more cuckoos in the nut house.' There was a sharp gasp, like the air escaping from a thousand balloons, then silence.

'This way,' said the Superintendent, leading the twins onwards, passing row after row of cell-like rooms and dormitories as they journeyed upwards.

'This is your hole,' she said at last, unlocking an iron door and shoving them inside.

'You don't have to push,' said Greta.

'Lots of things I don't have to do,' retorted the Superintendent. 'I don't have to feed you if I don't want to, do I?'

She laughed and slammed the door shut.

'There are probably rats,' whispered Greta, glancing around the damp and tiny room.

'At least rats might have eaten the cockroaches,' whimpered Feliks, as a tide of the shiny brown insects swept across the tiled floor. He climbed into bed and pulled the blanket over his head, only to discover that the cockroaches were also swarming across the bare mattress and under the pillow.

Greta kicked at the wall and the hatch in the door snapped open. Two black, beady eyes peered in, and the room was filled with the unmistakable aroma of garlic.

'You want me to tuck you in?' growled the Superintendent. Greta staggered backwards and mutely shook her head. 'Sweet dreams!'

There was a sharp and unpleasant bark of a laugh from the other side of the door, and the iron hatch was slammed shut. Greta stood and listened as the Superintendent's flat feet echoed along the corridor and clattered back down the spiral staircase.

Feliks turned over in bed. The blankets scratched like wire wool, and the shattered glass of the barred window let in an icy draught. Greta stood shivering, illuminated only by the pale moonlight, which filtered in between the bars. 'Maybe we could escape,' she whispered.

But Feliks shook his head. 'There's no way out,' he replied. 'It's hopeless.'

It seemed to Greta that she had barely fallen asleep, when a noise jolted her awake. She sat up in bed and listened. There were footsteps in the corridor and a rattle of keys at the cell door.

Greta climbed out of bed and shook Feliks awake.

'What is it?' he gasped. 'What's happening?'

Greta put her hand over Feliks's mouth as the door creaked slowly open. There stood the Superintendent. Greta shrank back into the corner of the room.

'There's nothing to fear,' said the Superintendent in a crackling whisper.

'You're lying,' said Greta.

'Would I lie?' replied the Superintendent. 'To a poppet like you?' Her face twitched uncertainly around the mouth, as though muscles were convulsing below the surface of her skin.

'Make her stop,' moaned Feliks, who half-feared the skin would peel away revealing an entirely new creature beneath. But the Superintendent's face settled into an expression that seemed at once familiar and at the same time entirely alien. She was attempting to smile.

'Get dressed, my little darlings,' said the Superintendent. 'I've got a surprise for you both. And put on your coats, you're going on an adventure.'

She waited outside in the corridor as the twins hastily dressed.

'Where's she taking us?' whispered Feliks, pulling on his muffler and shaking free a cockroach that had become entangled in a loose strand of wool.

'She's going to grind us to bits in a mincer, most probably,' said Greta. 'Then she'll serve us up as goulash to feed the other inmates.'

'Quickly now,' murmured the Superintendent, as the twins slowly emerged from their cell. 'I haven't got all night.' She led them along the passageway and down the cast-iron stairs. 'Not a noise now. Don't want the other maladjusted poppets getting sick with envy that you've got a new mother and they haven't.'

'A new mother?' said Greta in bewilderment. 'Who is she?'

'You'll find out soon enough,' answered the Superintendent.

'But we've only just got here,' said Feliks. 'Doesn't it

take a long time for orphans to find new parents?'

'I didn't say anything about a new father, did I?' said the Superintendent. 'Just a new mother.'

'What if we don't like her?' asked Greta, suddenly fearful that the Superintendent was about to pass them into the hands of a deranged lunatic.

'What if she doesn't like us?' added Feliks, who confidently predicted that matters were shortly to take a turn for the worse.

Greta stopped on a step. 'And what if we don't want to go?'

'But you do want to go, don't you, my little poppet?' replied the Superintendent, giving Greta a sharp prod in the ribs. 'Because it'll be the worse for you if you don't.' She led the twins into her office. 'Now sit there and shut up.' She departed, pulling the door closed behind her.

Feliks and Greta sat patiently awaiting the arrival of their new benefactor.

They soon heard voices outside the door.

'Whatever she's like she'll never be our mother,' said Greta obstinately. 'Aunt Gisela was our mother. And she wasn't even our mother.'

'Maybe whoever it is wants to use us as slaves,' said Feliks. 'That often happens. I've read about it in the newspaper.'

Suddenly the door opened and a tall woman stepped into the room, wrapping a silver fox fur tightly around her throat. The twins looked up in amazement.

There before them stood Olga Van Veenen.

CHAPTER ELEVEN

Olga Van Veenen smiled, revealing the whitest porcelain teeth the twins had ever seen. 'And here are the darling children,' she said, bending down and craning her neck to face the twins. 'I don't suppose you remember me?'

'Of course we remember you,' said Greta in awe. 'You're Olga Van Veenen.'

'Precious child,' said Olga. She gave a laugh, so high-pitched and glass-like it sounded like a chandelier swaying dangerously in a gust of wind.

'You'll need to sign in triplicate,' growled the Superintendent, pulling a bundle of papers from a drawer in her desk and holding out a fountain pen.

Olga waved the pen away, and took her own diamond-encrusted pen from her purse. She unscrewed the lid and signed the papers on the Superintendent's desk with a flourish, in bright purple ink. Greta stared hard at Olga's face; she wore purple eye shadow and lipstick, the precise colour of the ink with which she wrote.

With a flutter of her mascara-caked eyelashes, Olga replaced the lid of the fountain pen and turned to the Superintendent.

'Is that all?' she inquired.

'That's all,' grunted the Superintendent.

'Then I may take these charming children away from this wretched place?' asked Olga.

'Take them where you want,' said the Superintendent. 'No business of mine now, is it?'

'Please take us away,' pleaded Greta. 'She threatened to starve us.'

The Superintendent hugged Greta close, her hand tightly gripped over the girl's mouth. 'That's enough out of you, my poppet.'

'And this is how you treat your infant charges, is it?' demanded Olga, taking Greta's hand and gently prising her away from the Superintendent's clutches. 'You should be reported to the proper authorities.' When angry, Olga's voice had the power of a ship's horn on an ocean liner, and the Superintendent leant against her desk for support, as if knocked sideways by the force. Olga turned her eyes to the twins, globules of black mascara gluing her eyelashes into small black bunches.

Like the legs of a tarantula, thought Feliks.

'Such beautiful angels,' said Olga, gently brushing a gloved hand against Greta's cold, pale cheek. 'And orphans, too. My poor darlings.'

'Are you really going to take us away from here?' asked Greta.

Olga Van Veenen smiled and nodded. 'You'll never be unhappy, ever again,' she purred, 'for as long as you live.' She swung the fox-fur stole over her shoulder and whispered to the twins, 'I do not like your Superintendent one tiny bit.'

'I hope you'll both be very happy,' said the Superintendent sourly, resisting the urge to give the twins one last prod in the ribs.

It was raining outside and the twins hurried across the courtyard, following the quick footsteps of their new benefactor.

'The door, please, gatekeeper,' said Olga, waving grandly. The gatekeeper appeared from his office and the gates were pushed open.

'This way, my darlings,' said Olga.

Outside in the street, a gleaming black motor car was waiting for them.

'An Estler-Spitz Diabolo,' whispered Greta.

A tall man with closely cropped white hair stood beside the motor car, sheltering himself from the rain beneath a large pinstriped umbrella. He was outfitted in a grey chauffeur's uniform, with black leather gauntlets and a peaked cap. He was painfully thin, as thin as any of the carved alabaster skeletons flanking the grand tombs of the Schwartzgarten Municipal Cemetery. The skin was drawn so tight across his face it was easy to imagine the exact shape of the skull beneath.

'This is Valentin,' said Olga, as the human skeleton hurried to hold the vast canopy of the umbrella above the heads of the assembled party. 'He doesn't say much, which is a blessing, because what he does have to say is of little consequence.'

Valentin held the door as Olga climbed into the great motor car. He observed the twins with unblinking eyes as the rain beat heavily against the umbrella.

'Get in, my darlings!' said Olga, and the twins climbed in beside her, springing on the newly-waxed leather upholstery. A white ball of fur hurled itself from under the seat, a solid silver bell hanging round its neck.

'This is darling Chou-Chou,' said Olga, lifting the yapping Pekinese onto her lap. 'Aren't you, my precious?' Chou-Chou snapped wildly at Feliks and Greta. 'He's just trying to make friends, aren't you, darling?' Flecks of foam were forming at the corners of Chou-Chou's violently snapping mouth. He bared his teeth and gave a low growl. But Olga simply smiled and laughed, patting Chou-Chou's head and feeding him a liver biscuit from her purse which the dog scraped at noisily with his needle-sharp teeth. 'Now away, Valentin!'

Feliks and Greta gazed back at the bleak, grey walls of the Reformatory as the car sped away. Olga slipped the fox stole from her shoulders and removed her gloves, revealing purple fingernails exactly the same shade as her eyeshadow and lipstick and the ink in her fountain pen. She sank back against the leather cushions. 'And now we can relax.'

'Where are you taking us?' asked Feliks, suddenly struck by a pang of fear.

'To my town house, on the other side of Edvardplatz,'

said Olga, smiling. 'Your new home.' She reached out to take Greta's hand and the girl quickly adjusted the sleeve of her jacket to hide the threadbare pullover beneath. 'But first, my darlings, I think new clothes are in order, don't you?'

'You smell like Aunt Gisela,' said Greta, leaning close to Olga and shutting her eyes, as if to clutch at the ghost of her beloved aunt.

'Darling child,' said Olga. 'My favourite scent of all. Oil of petunia.'

It couldn't be happening, thought Greta. And yet it was. In the course of one night everything had slotted perfectly into place, or as perfectly as was possible without Aunt Gisela.

Olga nodded, and Greta was half-convinced that she had read her mind.

'It was Fate,' whispered Olga kindly. 'Fate smiled on you.'

The motor car slipped silently through the streets of Schwartzgarten. Though it was barely seven in the morning, market traders were already raising their stalls on the cobbles of Edvardplatz.

'To Bildstein and Bildstein, Valentin,' said Olga.

Valentin grunted and turned the steering wheel to the left.

'But the shop won't be open yet,' said Feliks.

Olga raised her beautifully curved eyebrows. 'Anything will open if you have the correct key,' she assured the boy.

The motor car pulled up outside Bildstein and Bildstein, a palatial department store on the corner of Bruckheimer Avenue and Beiderbeck Street. A commissionaire with golden epaulettes opened the door for Olga and the twins. The building was silent, but not deserted. An army of shop staff stood in readiness.

'Clothes, for the two children,' said Olga, clapping her hands in delight. 'Town clothes, and evening dress and Brammerhaus tweed for the country.'

'But they don't know our sizes,' said Feliks.

'I telephoned ahead,' Olga assured him. 'Everything is in order.'

The assistants scuttled away across the shop floor as Olga led the twins towards Bildstein and Bildstein's famous patisserie. The ceiling was painted azure blue, adorned with gilt cherubs. There was an ornamental fountain with a carved alabaster dolphin spouting water, and large golden koi carp swimming silently in the icy water below. A marble counter was piled high with glistening chocolate cakes, a brittle hazelnut and meringue torte and a sumptuous cloudberry cream gateau, decorated with curls of edible gold leaf.

'What would you like most of all, my darlings?' asked Olga, as a pastry chef in a tall white hat appeared behind the counter. But the choice was so great that the twins could only stare in awe at the desserts ranged before them. 'Two imperial caramel crèmes, I think,' said Olga, as she sat with the twins on a deep velvet couch.

The desserts were brought to the twins in frosted silver goblets, with long spoons of gold plate.

Feliks inspected the dessert closely, his nostrils quivering with delight. It was a creamy caramel mousse, topped with a foamy halo of piped cream and dusted with cinnamon. As he excavated it with his spoon, the mousse gave way to a silken core of delicious liquid caramel. It was the most perfect thing he had ever eaten, he decided. He was about to ask for the recipe – and then he remembered Aunt Gisela's vanilla pudding, and felt that he had betrayed her. He pushed the dessert away and refused to eat another mouthful.

'Too rich, my darling?' inquired Olga.

'Yes,' said Feliks, hanging his head unhappily.

'I bet I could eat another one,' said Greta, hungrily scraping the last of the caramel sauce from the sides of her goblet.

'I bet you couldn't,' said Olga with an indulgent smile.

'She gets sick if she eats too much,' said Feliks, and Greta kicked him hard in the shin.

'You can have pistachio nougat for breakfast, praline for lunch and chocolate truffles for supper.' Olga smiled. 'Whatever your hearts desire.'

The twins exchanged a glance. In the blink of an eye their lives had changed forever.

When they returned from the patisserie, the polished mahogany counter of the clothing department had been stacked with boxes. Greta and Feliks lifted lid after lid to reveal new pullovers and tweed jackets, evening clothes and countless pairs of shoes. Under Valentin's watchful eye, the boxes were carried out to the street by the regiment of shop assistants.

'One final stop,' said Olga, as they drove to the northernmost corner of Edvardplatz. The Estler-Spitz purred to a halt in front of the tall plum-coloured shop front of the chocolatier M. Kalvitas. It was not yet opening time, but a crowd of children had already gathered outside, pushing their noses to the window as Olga and the twins entered the shop.

They were served by the ancient Kalvitas himself, who entertained them with tales of long-ago battles, fighting at the side of Good Prince Eugene to free Schwartzgarten from the evil rule of Emeté Talbor. Kalvitas even lifted down the sword with which he had cut off the heads of assorted enemy generals and allowed Greta to chop up a chocolate praline log with the gleaming silver blade.

It was a wonderful shop, taller than it was wide, and Kalvitas nimbly climbed the steps to reach the uppermost shelves, pulling out trays of pistachio nougat, chocolate peanut croquant and cloudberry creams, which he packed into a box for Greta and Feliks. Olga Van Veenen picked out an enormous wooden crate of rose and cinnamon

Turkish delight, and a cardboard drum of macaroons for Chou-Chou.

Greta laughed. She had never seen so many sweetmeats in her life. Feliks, however, was consumed by unhappier thoughts. Sucking grimly on a lingonberry bonbon he could not shake the feeling that disaster lurked just around the corner.

'And a box of Pfefferberg's nougat marshmallows for the twins,' chirped Olga, as they were about to leave. 'In case they are hungry still.' She held the twins tightly by the hand, barely able to contain her excitement. 'And now, my angels. Now it is time for you to see your new home.'

CHAPTER TWELVE

〜◆◆◆◆◆〜

Olga's town house stood in the heart of Schwartzgarten, overlooking Edvardplatz. The building was so tall that it left the houses on either side in perpetual shadow.

'It's beautiful,' gasped Greta, staring up at the gabled roof towering high above them.

On either side of the doorway was a carved cherub face of polished marble, which seemed to smile down benignly at the twins.

Olga held her hand to one of the cold stone faces and smiled at Greta and Feliks. 'Now I have two cherubs of my very own.'

Valentin turned the key in the door and Olga Van Veenen led the twins inside.

'It's too small, of course,' said Olga as Greta and Feliks stepped into the entrance hall, 'but I call it home.'

Valentin grunted and returned to the motor car to carry in the boxes of clothes and chocolates.

The twins had never seen a house so large. Every

footstep they took in the grand hallway echoed back at them from the high vaulted glass ceiling. The floor was an elaborate mosaic, with the name 'Olga Van Veenen' spelled out in many thousands of purple tiles running the length of the hall. A full-length portrait of the children's new guardian hung at the far end of the passageway.

Bouquets of red roses overflowed from vases that stood in every niche and on every table.

'From my adoring public,' said Olga, snapping the head off a bright scarlet rose, sniffing it and throwing it to the floor, where Chou-Chou snapped up the petals hungrily. 'Come with me,' chirped Olga, as the heels of her shoes clattered over the mosaic floor. 'This, my darlings,' she continued, as she swept through a doorway at the end of the hall, 'this is where I write my books.'

The twins followed their benefactor into the room. The front cover of every one of Olga Van Veenen's three hundred books hung in golden frames from the wall.

'This is where my delightful characters spring to life,' said Olga, gesturing to a carved mahogany desk on which stood an elegant portable typewriter, with purple keys.

The twins were finding it difficult to keep up with

their guardian; she had already turned on her heel, wafting along the hallway and divesting herself of her fur coat, which Valentin dutifully took from her.

'Follow me, my darlings,' said Olga. 'So much to see.'

She led the twins into the drawing room, with its ornate plaster ceiling and wallpaper of purple brocaded silk. There were so many vases of roses that the aroma was almost overpowering. Among the flowers, on elegant cut-glass cake stands, were soaring towers of brightly coloured macaroons and deep bowls of sugared almonds. A golden ormolu clock took pride of place on an enormous fireplace of polished marble. The mechanism whirred as the clock chimed the quarter-hour.

'Cloisonné,' said Olga Van Veenen, 'I'm a great collector.' She waved her hand vaguely, indicating the other cloisonné objets d'art which glittered in the morning light. 'It was originally introduced by the ancient Chinese. It's made of a honeycomb of intricate chambers, forged from gold or silver and filled with brightly coloured enamels.'

The chiming timepiece was flanked by a glittering cloisonné peacock on the left, and a clockwork cuckoo in a golden cage on the right. Olga reached across to a crocodile-skin box with silver feet, which stood on a low table. She took out a cigarette with a purple tip and held it to her purple lips. She lit the cigarette from a cloisonné cigarette lighter, shaped as a bear standing on its hind legs.

'Cigarettes can kill,' said Feliks.

'How charming,' said Olga Van Veenen, blowing a smoke ring that hovered like a choking halo above Feliks's head. She offered a bowl of sugared almonds to the twins.

'We can't eat almonds,' said Feliks. 'We're allergic.'

'Our tongues swell up,' said Greta.

'Then we die,' concluded Feliks.

'Of course,' said Olga, replacing the bowl. 'How foolish of me.'

———

Greta and Feliks spent the morning and afternoon alone together, as Olga Van Veenen typed away behind the closed door of her study. The twins had been left in the drawing room with a pile of Olga's books, and the box of Pfefferberg's nougat marshmallows from Kalvitas's shop.

As Feliks leafed through the pages of *Thirteen Deaths At Midnight*, a photograph slipped out from between the pages. It was the photograph of a young boy with a pug nose and freckles. On the back, written in purple ink, was the name: Friedrich. The photograph was remarkable for one reason alone: it had been crossed out very neatly in thick, red ink.

'That's strange,' said Feliks, holding up the photograph. 'Why do you think Olga has this?'

Greta shrugged. 'I don't know,' she said. 'Maybe it was someone who didn't like her books.'

Feliks replaced the photograph between the pages of the book and helped himself to another Pfefferberg marshmallow.

———◆———

'I don't know if I like Olga,' said Feliks, as the twins washed for an early supper. 'What do we know about her anyway?'

'She travels on ocean liners, and steam trains and airships,' said Greta. 'That's the important information. Anything else we'll find out later on.'

'What if she's a murderer?' said Feliks.

'You read too many newspapers,' said Greta. 'You always think everybody is a murderer.'

'Then it's logical that one day I'll be right,' sighed Feliks. 'And then you'll wish you'd listened to me.'

Greta dried her hands. 'You don't read enough books,' she said.

'I do read books,' replied Feliks.

'Recipe books,' said Greta. 'But not adventure books. So you don't know what happens in real life. Aunt Gisela died, that was very bad. But now Olga Van Veenen has come to rescue us. That's what always happens in books. Something very bad happens, then something very good.'

'It's not what happens in the newspapers,' said Feliks. 'Bad things happen then continue to happen.'

'I hope you are settling in, my darlings?' asked Olga as Feliks and Greta returned to the drawing room. She rang the bell and Valentin loomed into view. 'Cocoa and pastries for the twins,' she said, smiling sweetly. Valentin grunted and headed for the kitchen.

'I don't think he likes us,' said Greta.

'Valentin doesn't like anybody much,' replied Olga. 'Sometimes I don't think he even likes me.'

After a supper of cocoa and plum pastries and pistachio nougat, Olga led the twins up the sweeping marble staircase to their new bedroom.

'I hope you'll be comfortable,' said Olga, swinging open the door.

It was an enormous room, with a bed at either end, and large windows that looked out across Edvardplatz. The blankets had been pulled back, with a pale violet nightdress for Greta, and mauve flannel pyjamas for Feliks, each with their names picked out in gold and silver thread.

'Why are there bars on the windows?' asked Feliks suspiciously.

'It's for your own safety,' insisted Olga, 'because if you can't get out of your room, then nobody can get in.'

Feliks was not convinced and was about to say as much when Greta silenced him with a glare.

'Good night, my darlings,' whispered Olga as she kissed the twins on the forehead and tucked them into bed.

It was impossible not to be impressed by the softness of the cotton sheets and goose feather pillows after the coarse blankets of the Schwartzgarten Reformatory for Maladjusted Children the night before. The twins fell instantly asleep.

Greta and Feliks slept so soundly that at eight o'clock the following morning they had still failed to emerge from their bedroom. Even the sonorous boom of the Schwartzgarten clock failed to wake them from their slumbers.

It was Feliks who eventually woke first.

'What time is it?' he gasped, sitting up suddenly.

Greta murmured and rolled over in her bed at the far end of the room, pulling a pillow over her head.

Feliks ran across to his sister, slipping on the polished floor and almost crashing into a pile of toys that had been arranged at the foot of the bed. 'Wake up!' he cried, shaking Greta so hard that she sat up with a jolt.

'What is it?' she gasped, a nameless dread suddenly clawing at her spine.

'It's almost nine o'clock,' said Feliks. 'We've slept too late.'

They dressed quickly in the new clothes that had been hung in their wardrobes and together they made their way downstairs, treading gently on the marble steps for fear they would be caught and punished for their laziness.

Their hopes of passing into the drawing room

undetected were dashed. There, in the doorway of her study, stood Olga Van Veenen.

'We're sorry,' blurted Feliks.

'We didn't mean to oversleep,' said Greta, standing protectively in front of her brother.

'Oversleep?' said Olga, her eyes narrowing quizzically. Suddenly she threw back her head and laughed until her eyes began to water and dark rivulets of mascara coursed down her face.

'You can sleep as late as you want, my angels,' she trilled. 'You can do whatever you want, whenever you want.'

'But won't we have chores?' asked Feliks. 'To earn our keep, I mean?'

'I'll tell you a little secret,' said Olga, whispering to the twins with a conspiratorial smile. 'That's why we have Valentin.'

'So what do we do?' said Greta

'How do you normally entertain yourselves?' asked Olga.

'We used to study,' replied Feliks. 'Aunt Gisela taught us maths and reading. And how to bake cakes.'

Olga raised her eyebrows. 'My poor darlings,' she purred. 'Well, you need never study again as long as you live under my roof.'

'But how are we going to learn things?' asked Feliks.

Olga looked puzzled. 'What sort of things were you expecting to learn?' she inquired.

'Algebra and calculus,' said Feliks. 'That sort of thing.'

Olga stared hard at the twins, as though they were afflicted by some form of mental delirium. 'Must you?' she asked.

'Yes, we must,' insisted Feliks.

'Yes, yes. I suppose you're right,' agreed Olga. 'I will see to it at once.'

———

The twins enjoyed an untroubled week with Olga Van Veenen. She was a kind and interested guardian, who wished to know everything there was to know about their lives with Aunt Gisela. Every day, she took them to Kalvitas's shop on Edvardplatz, talking to Greta and Feliks about their tragic lives as they sipped from steaming mugs of caramel hot chocolate.

Though their time with Olga passed quickly and happily, the twins were disturbed to read in *The Informant* that following the death of Von Merhart, the Cinema of Blood was to close its doors forever. More worrying to the twins, the newspaper also reported that overnight the monster actors had disappeared. Bullfrog, Vladek and Gabor, China Doll, the Blind Butcher and Doctor Kessler; it seemed they had vanished from the face of the earth.

Olga was as good as her word and arranged for a tutor to educate the twins.

'This,' said Olga, when a motor car arrived punctually outside the house on the Wednesday morning, 'is Mr Tantalus. Your tutor.'

Tantalus was a small man with pince-nez spectacles, a homburg hat and a neatly clipped beard.

'Good morning,' said the tutor, making a low bow to the children. His eyes seemed to sparkle.

The lessons took place in the dining room. But the twins were surprised to discover that there were to be no classes in mathematics, history or languages.

'In today's lesson we will deal with varieties of poisonous fungus,' said Mr Tantalus, on the morning of his first day's teaching. 'Please turn to page seventeen,' he continued, passing the twins two slim volumes devoted to the identification of mushrooms and toadstools.

Greta and Feliks opened their books.

Feliks stared hard at a coloured print of a large, yellow-capped mushroom. 'The death cap toadstool,' he murmured.

'Ah,' said Mr Tantalus. 'The death cap. Indeed.'

'Is it true,' asked Feliks, 'that if you eat a death cap, you die?'

'Quite true, quite true,' said Mr Tantalus.

'In pain and agony?' asked Greta, her eyes gleaming.

'That is quite correct,' said Mr Tantalus, clapping his hands together. 'In pain and agony. And what is more,' he concluded, 'there is no known antidote.'

The following morning, matters turned to espionage.

'Today's lesson,' said Mr Tantalus. 'How to decipher hidden codes.'

'You're going to teach us about secret messages?' asked Feliks in surprise.

'Indeed I am,' replied Mr Tantalus, placing a bottle on the table and two quill pens.

Greta frowned. 'What's inside the bottle?' she asked.

'Lemon juice,' explained Mr Tantalus. 'Invisible ink. This is the old way of passing messages without risk of detection. Now dip your quills, and write your names on the paper provided.'

The twins did as they were instructed, and scratched out their names on the paper with the sharpened tip of their quill pens.

'Very good,' said Mr Tantalus. 'Next we wait for the invisible ink to dry.'

As soon as the lemon juice was dry to the touch, Mr Tantalus lit two candles. 'And now,' said the tutor. 'Hold the paper carefully above the flame.'

Greta laughed and Feliks watched open-mouthed as their names were magically revealed, as if written in brown ink.

'And that,' said Mr Tantalus, 'is the simplest way of concealing a secret message.'

After lessons had finished for the day, the twins went for a walk to Edvardplatz. Olga, who was busy working in her study, did not accompany them. A small touring fair had been erected on the cobbles, a ramshackle assortment of tents and sideshows that occupied the eastern corner of the square. There was a smell of sugar in the air, of hot caramel nuts and gingerbread. Greta and Feliks had the uneasy feeling that they were being watched.

'Win all you can knock down!' cried a large woman, with a cigarette hanging from her lower lip. Behind her was a stall, lined with tinplate toys and boxes of chocolates. 'Corks or pellets?' she said, pointing to the rifles. Feliks shook his head politely.

The woman leant forward and whispered hoarsely to the twins. 'The House of Terrors, then,' she said, slipping an envelope into the palm of Greta's hand. 'Maybe that's more to your liking?' And with that she turned and shouted out as before, 'Win all you can knock down! Corks or pellets!'

Confused, the twins moved on, passing the Palace of Illusions, and stopped outside the House of Terrors. 'Well?' said Feliks impatiently as Greta opened the envelope. 'What's inside?'

Greta held up a small scrap of paper.

Meet me inside the House of Terrors. Come alone.

The outer walls of the House of Terrors had been carved to resemble a row of skeletal figures, and an enormous skull leered out above the entrance, with sinister eyes illuminated by the flickering flames of two large gas lamps. The twins paid a crown each from the weekly allowance of five imperial crowns that Olga had provided, and took an anxious step inside.

The House of Terrors did not live up to its name.

'It's not very terrifying,' whispered Greta, brushing past a wooden skeleton so its bones trembled and clattered.

'Whoever wanted us to come here must have a sense of humour,' observed Feliks, staring in amusement at the wax figure of a vampire that had melted in the heat of a gas lamp.

'It's a waste of two crowns,' replied Greta bitterly. 'We could have spent it on pistachio nougat.'

'Perhaps it was only a joke, after all?' said Feliks. 'If somebody did want to meet us here, where are they?'

They turned a corner and gasped. There before them stood the only genuinely startling wax figure in the House of Terrors. It was dressed in a long wig, with protruding teeth and a face pockmarked with livid red pustules.

'It's just another waxwork,' said Greta, recovering herself. She gave the figure a hard push. But to Greta's horror the wax figure pushed back and reached out to grip the twins in its enormous hands.

CHAPTER THIRTEEN

G reta was just opening her mouth to scream when a familiar voice whispered urgently, 'It's me.'

Greta closed her mouth and a thin whisper escaped her lips: 'Morbide!'

'But we thought you were in prison,' said Feliks.

'I was,' said Morbide. He attempted a smile, but it was no good.

'Did they let you out?' asked Greta, watching the man closely.

'In a manner of speaking,' said Morbide. 'I escaped. But we can't talk here.'

'Where can we go?' asked Feliks. 'Won't the police be hunting for you?'

'If we're careful we can keep out of their way,' said Morbide. He guided the twins out through a hidden doorway disguised as the entrance to a mausoleum and along a passageway lined with shelves of wax limbs and glass eyes. He removed the false teeth and the long black wig, and slipped on an overcoat that hung from a rusted nail. 'We must be quiet as the grave,' he whispered, pulling on a hat and lowering the brim so it covered his eyes. He opened a second door that led out onto the cobbles of Edvardplatz, behind the House of Terrors. 'We'll go to Mrs Moritz. She knows I'm here.'

———

It took them over an hour to walk from Edvardplatz to the Old Town, and night closed in around them. Morbide insisted that they should slink through the shadows, avoiding every policeman and passer-by until they returned to the familiar surroundings of Donmerplatz.

Morbide tapped three times at the window of Mrs Moritz's shop and the door swung open a crack.

'Morbide?' whispered Mrs Moritz. 'Is that you?'

'Yes,' replied Morbide. 'And I've brought company.'

There was a muffled squeak. 'Not the police?" panted Mrs Moritz.

'No,' said Morbide. 'Friends.'

The door opened wide.

'Come in, quickly,' whispered Mrs Moritz, herding Morbide and the twins inside the shop and locking the door behind them. 'Feliks and Greta,' she gasped, 'is it really you?'

The twins grinned.

'And your clothes! Look at your clothes! If your aunt could see you now, which she can't, dead in the grave as she is, poor dear departed soul.' Mrs Moritz hastily pulled down the blinds. 'Were you followed?' she whispered.

'I don't think so,' replied Morbide. 'It's not safe for me to walk around in the daylight,' he explained to the twins.

'In case you're recognised,' said Feliks.

Morbide nodded.

'So how did you escape?' asked Greta, almost bursting under the weight of the question.

'It was like this—' began Morbide, only to be interrupted by a sudden fluttering noise from behind the counter and a wild squawk, as a bright red parrot took to the air.

'Karloff!' cried Feliks. The bird circled above the twins. He settled briefly on the counter, hopped from foot to foot and scooped up a beak full of bird seed that Mrs Moritz had placed out of reach of the cats.

'He flew back here to the shop the night you were

taken,' said Mrs Moritz. 'I didn't know where you'd gone, so I've been keeping him safe for you.'

Karloff took to the air again, squawking loudly and spilling millet from his beak, which showered down around the twins and bounced from the floor.

'If I ate half as well as that parrot, life would be good,' moaned Mrs Moritz. 'And the fatter he gets, the more my cats go for him, don't they?' she continued, gently shaking off a ginger tom that was pawing at her leg and scratching long ladders in her stockings. 'I can't tell you the money I spend out on millet.'

'Spend out on millet!' squawked Karloff.

Mrs Moritz pulled back the blinds and squinted outside. Two police constables stood on the opposite side of the street, questioning a man in a greasy grey vest.

'Police,' hissed Mrs Moritz to Morbide. 'You'd better get out before they find you here.'

'Then we must have been seen,' said Morbide. 'Nowhere's safe for long.'

Mrs Moritz pulled back the curtain to her consulting room, and hurried Morbide inside. 'The window's not too far off the ground,' she whispered, as a loud knock was heard from the door of the shop.

'Coming!' she called. 'Can't a woman get a bit of peace without someone trying to shake the door off its hinges?'

'Police!' shouted a voice.

'Don't care who you are,' screeched Mrs Moritz as she attempted to shove Morbide through the tiny window at the back of the consulting room to the safety of the alley outside. 'A door's a door. Damage my earthly goods and I'll wring your necks for you, police or no police.'

Morbide had dropped squarely, though unsteadily, to his feet.

'Luck of a cat!' said Mrs Moritz, much impressed.

Morbide smiled sadly up at the twins. 'You'd better go back to your guardian,' he whispered. 'It'll be safer for you.'

The twins had almost forgotten about Olga Van Veenen.

Greta shook her head. 'We want to come with you,' she said. 'We can't lose you again so soon.'

Feliks nodded in agreement.

'Whatever you're going to do, do it quickly,' hissed Mrs Moritz.

Morbide reached up to help the twins out of the

window. Karloff landed on Feliks's head, digging his claws into the boy's scalp and refusing to let go.

Once more the police hammered against the shop door.

'I'll stall them,' said Mrs Moritz, bustling through to the shop. 'Now hurry and don't stop for anyone.'

As Morbide and the twins quickly made their way along the alleyway, they could hear Mrs Moritz's voice in the distance.

'What do you mean "escaped murderer"?' she demanded. 'Think I'd let an escaped murderer in here? Tell you what I'll do, I'll make a good strong pot of coffee and I'll tell your fortunes – that might turn up your murderer for you. No, don't sit there, the cat's just messed on it. I'll get a cloth and wipe you down.'

If Mrs Moritz had one talent in life, it was a talent for conversation. By the time the two police constables weaved out onto the street, they were covered in cat hairs, full of apple brandy, and had had their fortunes told twice. Mrs Moritz supplied two possible explanations for the disappearance of Morbide; he was either living in a hut on the shores of Lake Taneva, or he had grown a moustache and disguised himself as the Inspector of Police. Sobering up on the street outside, the constables were reluctant to return to the Department of Police to propose either of Mrs Moritz's suggestions.

Meanwhile, Morbide and the twins had safely fled the alleyway. Karloff had disentangled himself from Feliks's hair and had settled happily on the boy's shoulder. They negotiated their way to Death's Doorstep and along the narrow street to the Cinema of Blood. The building was deserted and the gaping mouth, which had once provided entrance to the cinema, was boarded shut.

'Follow me,' said Morbide, beckoning to the twins as he turned off into a side alley that led alongside the cinema. 'If we go in at the front I might be spotted.'

The twins made their way carefully past piles of rubbish where rats squealed and darted. Morbide sighed miserably under his breath but turned and smiled at Greta, who let out an involuntary squeak as she accidentally stepped on the tail of a particularly hefty rat. Karloff gave a subdued squawk and nibbled nervously at Feliks's ear.

'This is it,' said Morbide, arriving outside a boarded-up window of the cinema. 'This is the way in.' He smiled again, but his heart ached with sadness. He pulled back the boards and dragged an old crate to the wall so Greta and Feliks could climb in through the window. Following behind, Morbide pulled the boards back into place and stood with the twins in the darkness.

'The electricity's gone,' said Morbide, as he took three candle stumps from a box beside the now-empty ticket booth. Lighting the candles, he led the twins into the very bowels of the deserted cinema. 'This way,' he said, guiding them through a doorway and behind the cinema screen.

'This way,' murmured Karloff.

It was a miserable place. The walls were piled high with rusting tins of movie film. The roof leaked and rotting paper and mounds of rat droppings littered the floor. Morbide had fashioned a bed from an old wooden door, supported at each corner by three stacked tins of film, with another tower of tins serving as a rudimentary table and a portable gas stove and lantern on top.

'You've been living here?' said Greta in disbelief.

Morbide nodded sadly and lit the lantern. 'It isn't much,' he said, a faint smile flickering briefly across his face, 'but it's home.'

He prepared an early supper for the twins on the tiny stove, while Karloff pecked hungrily at the scuttling roaches.

'You didn't really kill Von Merhart, did you?' asked Feliks as Morbide stirred a pan with the handle of a bug swatter that he carried for protection.

'Of course he didn't,' said Greta. 'Did you, Morbide?'

Morbide shook his head. 'No,' he replied. 'But someone wants to make it look as though I did. The police are saying I killed the Brandberg Brothers as well.'

'Who are the Brandberg Brothers?' asked Feliks.

'They had a construction firm,' explained Morbide. 'They made sets and props for the movie studios. Seems they ended up the same way as Von Merhart. With two holes in their necks and their factory burned to the ground.'

Greta stared hard at Morbide's head; it was red and blistered with fleabites. 'Isn't there anywhere else you can stay?' she asked.

'I'm a hunted man. You saw that,' said Morbide, handing Greta and Feliks a plate of boiled potatoes, a tin of pickled herrings and a spoon. 'At least the police aren't going to come sniffing round here. They'd get a shock if they did,' he added, lifting a curious rat from the tabletop and dropping it gently onto the floor. 'Rats I can live with. It's the cockroaches that make my life a misery. And that's all Von Merhart's fault.'

Morbide explained that the cockroach infestation had been encouraged by Von Merhart, in an attempt to make the Cinema of Blood more horrific. Morbide remembered well the day the first crate of cockroaches had been delivered to the cinema. Rashly, Von Merhart had also purchased a crate of exotic spiders, which turned out to be more poisonous than he had anticipated. Within days the spiders had either eaten each other or been stung to death, but the roaches had multiplied with each passing year and they showed no signs of departing. Morbide's cockroach traps, which he baited with lingonberry syrup and arsenic, were full of insects: some dead, some still twitching or struggling to escape. But most of the creatures had grown immune to the poison. If anything, they seemed to be thriving on the arsenic and had increased in size. Morbide shuddered as the shadowy creatures scuttled in and out of a rat hole in the wall, just visible beyond the halo of lamplight.

At night, Morbide confided, he slept with his blanket over his head, so that roaches could not drop into his ears. Though they had only spent one night in the roach-ridden Reformatory, it was a horror the twins could well imagine and they sympathised with their friend.

'You'd better go,' said Morbide at last, as Feliks and Greta finished their supper. 'Van Veenen will want to know where you are. She'll be worried.'

Feliks jolted. It was as if a spike of ice had been driven through his stomach. He felt unaccountably fearful of a return to Olga's town house, and try as he might he could not shake off a clawing sense of dread.

'But what about the others?' asked Greta. 'What about China Doll?'

'I've lost her, haven't I?' said Morbide, taking pity on a passing rat and feeding it a scrap of pickled herring. 'I was taken to prison and when I returned, she'd gone. I've looked, but there's no sign of her. Nothing. It's as if she never lived.'

'We'll help you find her,' said Greta. Morbide raised his head and a flicker of hope passed across his face.

'It's got to be easier if three of us are looking,' said Feliks. 'We'll come back tomorrow morning,'

Taking Karloff with them, the twins left Morbide to fend off the cockroaches, and caught the tram back across the river and into Edvardplatz. It was long after supper by the time they arrived home, and they crept silently into the hall of Olga's town house.

'What are we going to do about Karloff?' whispered Feliks.

'Do about Karloff!' murmured the parrot.

Greta quickly held her hand over his beak.

'If we can just get him upstairs,' said Greta quietly, hiding Karloff beneath her coat. 'Then we can plan what to do next.'

'I thought you were lost to me, my darlings,' said a voice as Greta took her first step on the staircase.

The twins turned to see Olga, silhouetted in the doorway of her study. They stared guiltily at their guardian.

'You don't need to keep any secrets from me,' continued Olga, as Chou-Chou followed his mistress into the hall.

Before Greta had the chance to utter a single word,

Karloff emerged from beneath her coat. He squawked and shook himself, soaring up towards the glass ceiling. Lazily, Chou-Chou pawed at the air, then gave up and trotted back into the study.

Olga stretched out her hand and Karloff obediently came to rest, perching on her diamond bracelet. 'What a beautiful creature,' said Olga, stroking the back of Karloff's neck.

Karloff clicked his tongue appreciatively and hopped from foot to foot, but did not speak a word.

'He doesn't say anything?' asked Olga.

'He does,' said Feliks defensively.

'But only when he wants to,' added Greta.

'What is his name?' asked Olga, allowing the bird to nip gently at her fingers.

'Karloff,' said Greta. 'He was Aunt Gisela's parrot.'

Olga smiled and nodded. 'Karloff,' she repeated. 'A very good name. Well, Karloff, perhaps you know why the twins did not return home to me in time for their supper?'

'We went for a walk to Edvardplatz,' stammered Feliks.

Olga held a finger to her lips. 'No more, my darling,' she said softly. 'Sometimes it is important for us to keep our secrets.'

'Keep our secrets!' cried Karloff, flapping his wings and flying from Olga's hand to settle on Feliks's shoulder.

'We've never had a parrot in the house before,' said Olga.

'Do you want to take him away from us?' asked Feliks unhappily.

'Take him away?' repeated Olga in surprise. 'But of course you must keep him, my darlings. All children should have a pet animal.' She clapped her hands and laughed. 'How delightful. Now up to bed, my precious twins. You need sleep for whatever adventures you have in store tomorrow.'

Chapter Fourteen

The next morning, as arranged, the twins met Morbide outside the House of Terrors. It was a Saturday and there were to be no lessons with Mr Tantalus for the day.

Morbide was heavily disguised, with a grey wig, false nose, beard and spectacles.

Together they walked the streets of Schwartzgarten, searching for any sign of China Doll. Karloff soared high above them, squawking happily as he stretched his wings.

They visited the lodging house in the Old Town where China Doll had once lived, but she had been thrown out days before and had not left a forwarding address.

'It's hopeless,' groaned Morbide. 'We'll never find her again. She's lost to me.'

'We can't stop looking,' said Greta. 'She's got to be out there somewhere. And if she is, we'll find her.'

They spent the entire morning walking the city streets, but China Doll was nowhere to be seen. Morbide's spirits were flagging, so the twins decided to use the last of their allowance to take their friend for cakes at the patisserie in the department store of Bildstein and Bildstein. Reluctantly, Morbide allowed himself to be led.

But the doors were blocked by a large crowd, which had assembled in front of the department store. They were gazing in through the enormous plate-glass window at a tall and beautiful woman as she stared forlornly back at them. At her feet was a sign:

BILDSTEIN AND BILDSTEIN PROUDLY PRESENT THE

MARVELLOUS MOVING MANNEQUIN

Morbide, who was tall enough to peer across the crowd, gave a low gasp.

'China Doll.'

'Is it really her?' whispered Feliks.

Morbide did not utter a word, but gathered the twins up in his arms and gently pushed his way to the front of the crowd. China Doll wore a long wig of auburn curls, and her face had been painted with rouge and lipstick to give colour to her ashen features. She looked more like a doll than ever. She was dressed in a long gown of yellow silk and stood sadly beside a plaster pillar. A bell chimed from inside the shop, and China Doll altered her position, now sitting down at an elegant table, piled high with wax fruit. Morbide pressed his hands against the window, staring open-mouthed at the vision before him. His lips moved, but barely a sound escaped them.

'China Doll,' he mouthed.

They waited the remainder of the afternoon on the freezing pavement until the department store closed its doors for the evening and the Marvellous Moving Mannequin was allowed to leave.

As China Doll emerged, Greta saw that her own clothes were threadbare and patched. She wrapped a scarf tight around her bony shoulders to keep out the cold. She nodded to the twins, and smiled sadly at Morbide.

'China Doll,' said Morbide, taking her hand in his and kissing it gently. 'That things should have come to this.'

'They don't pay me much,' murmured China Doll, wiping the make-up from her cheeks. 'I can't complain though. It keeps food on the table.'

'But not much, I think,' said Morbide. 'We need to feed you up.'

'How did you find me?' asked China Doll.

Morbide motioned to Feliks and Greta. 'I had help,' he said.

He led the twins and China Doll over the cobbles of Edvardplatz to Kalvitas's chocolate shop, still keeping to the shadows. All the time he watched China Doll from the corner of his eye, anxious not to offend her by staring directly. She was even thinner and paler than ever and Morbide was determined to rectify this at all costs.

'You need to eat,' whispered Morbide, taking care not to be overheard and pulling the scarf around his mouth to avoid being recognised. He heaped China Doll's plate with macaroons, paid for with the money he had earned at the House of Terrors, money he had been saving for such an occasion. 'If you don't eat there'll be nothing left of you.'

'I'll just fade into the shadows,' said China Doll quietly.

'Have a Pfefferberg's marshmallow,' said Greta.

China Doll peeled back the gold foil and sighed. It would clearly take time for Morbide to convince her that things would still turn out for the best.

'We should go,' said Feliks.

Greta nodded.

Outside, the twins waved through the window of the chocolate shop, smiling as Morbide held China Doll's delicate fingers, and gently pressed another Pfefferberg's marshmallow into the palm of her hand.

———◆———

That night, as Greta descended the staircase for supper, Feliks ran in with the late edition of *The Informant*.

'There was a police raid on the Cinema of Blood,' he panted. 'They've arrested Morbide.'

'Nobody knew he was there,' moaned Greta. 'Nobody but you, me and Mrs Moritz.'

'And China Doll,' added Feliks.

'He'll think it was us,' said Greta, her eyes wide with alarm. 'He'll think that we told the police.'

'Well, somebody told them,' said Feliks. 'If it wasn't us, who else could it have been?'

This was a good question, and Greta pondered matters.

'My darlings,' said Olga as she entered the hall with Valentin and beckoned the twins into the dining room.

'I've just heard troubling news about your friend Morbide.'

Greta hung her head and Olga stared questioningly at her. 'Did you know that Morbide was here in Schwartzgarten?'

'Yes,' replied Greta in a whisper. 'We visited him.'

'If only you had told me before, my darlings,' said Olga, sitting at the dining table, 'perhaps we could have done something to save him from his unhappy fate.'

'What will happen to him?' asked Feliks.

'I hardly dare tell you,' said Olga, stroking Chou-Chou, who had climbed up onto her lap. 'You must prepare yourselves for the very worst. Mr Morbide will almost certainly live out the rest of his days behind bars.'

'But Morbide is innocent,' said Feliks.

'That may well be,' replied Olga. 'But in the eyes of the law, an escape from prison is as good as an admission of guilt.'

'Is there nothing we can do?' asked Greta.

'We shall see,' said Olga. 'I will do the best I can, my darlings. My very best.'

Olga Van Veenen spent the afternoon telephoning from her study, first to the Inspector of Police and then to the Governor of Schwartzgarten, pleading for Morbide's release.

But it was no good. Even with the celebrated Olga Van Veenen pleading in his defence, Morbide was returned to prison.

—◆—

The days passed slowly. There was no news of Morbide and the twins pictured him alone in his cell, once more separated from China Doll.

A week later the twins were instructed to dress in formal clothes for dinner.

'We shall visit the Old Chop House,' said Olga with a twinkle in her eye. 'It might cheer you both up, my darlings.'

Feliks wore a black tailcoat and a starched wing collar, which dug uncomfortably into his neck. Greta wore a black dress, embroidered with diamonds in the shape of a peacock. It seemed to Feliks that his sister had even begun to dress like Olga Van Veenen, and this was unsettling.

As Greta passed Olga's door on her way downstairs,

the girl's guardian called softly to her. Olga sat at her dressing table, powdering her face.

'Darling, do come in,' she said, turning to her visitor.

Greta crossed the floor as Olga applied raven-black mascara and eyebrow pencil. The aroma of oil of petunia hung deliciously in the air.

'Do you think I'm very beautiful, child?' asked Olga.

Greta stared into the mirror at her guardian's reflection. She nodded.

Olga observed the girl closely. 'You've got good bones,' she said, draping a diamond choker around her beautiful pale throat. She opened a drawer in the dressing table and took out a velvet box, which she gently pressed into Greta's hands. Inside was the intertwined pin of the Van Veenen Adventure Society.

'I've already got a pin,' said Greta.

'But not with real diamonds,' said Olga, removing the pin from the box and fastening it to Greta's dress.

Greta smiled.

'Now run along, child,' said Olga, 'Feliks will be waiting for you.'

As the twins descended the marble staircase, Valentin

was outside in the street, starting the engine of the motor car.

Chou-Chou barked and yapped excitedly.

'Stop that at once, Chou-Chou,' snapped Olga, and the dog gave a mournful whine as it followed her.

It was a cold night and the streets were empty. Valentin drew up alongside the Old Chop House, and the engine purred to a halt. As Olga and the twins climbed from the motor car a tall man, with a smooth bald head, emerged from inside the building, pulling on a pair of leather motoring gauntlets. He wore a long coat of Brammerhaus tweed and gleaming black riding boots. He stared admiringly at the Estler-Spitz and was about to take a step forward when he caught sight of Olga and remained rooted to the spot. He smiled, though it clearly caused him discomfort to do so.

'What a coincidence to see you at the Old Chop House tonight, my dear sister.'

'What are you doing here, Sebastian?' replied Olga icily.

'I am in the city on business,' replied the man. 'I had intended to visit the Cinema of Blood but alas, I discovered that the place has been boarded shut. So instead I came here to dine.'

The twins stared at the man in curiosity.

'My name is Count Sebastian Van Veenen,' said the man with a low bow. 'And who are these delightful children?'

Feliks smiled. 'I'm Feliks,' he said, 'and this is my sister, Greta.'

Count Sebastian took Greta's hand. 'You will be a great beauty,' he whispered. 'But don't let the other girls know that I told you that, they will be quite puce with envy.'

'Is that all, Sebastian?' said Olga.

'Alas, my sister treats me as something of a pariah,' said Count Sebastian to the twins with a mischievous sparkle in his eye. Gently, he ran his index finger across the immaculately polished bonnet of the motor car. 'A new Estler-Spitz, I see.'

'The Diabolo,' replied Olga. 'Adapted to my very own specifications. A one-off. But now it's getting cold and I don't want the twins catching a chill.'

'Of course not,' replied her brother. 'Well, goodbye,

dear children,' said Count Sebastian, waving a gauntleted hand in their direction as Olga led the twins inside.

'It's best that you never associate with Count Sebastian,' said Olga.

'But why?' asked Greta. 'He seemed nice.'

'Looks are almost always deceptive,' replied Olga. 'Just read one of my books. The villains are always charming to begin with.'

This was true, but Greta persisted. 'You mean Count Sebastian is a villain?' she asked.

Olga inhaled sharply. 'It's very hard for me to talk about it,' she said. 'Sebastian brought shame upon the Van Veenen family.'

'So he is a villain,' said Greta triumphantly.

'My darlings,' confided Olga. 'What I have to tell you is shocking. But then, you seem the unshockable types. Count Sebastian is a murderer.'

'He didn't look like a murderer,' said Feliks.

Greta shrugged. 'Murderers never do look like murderers,' she said. 'That's how you can tell.'

Valentin ushered Greta and Feliks into the private dining room of the Van Veenen family, where a candelabrum flickered with candlelight.

'That was my father,' said Olga, pointing her finger at a painting that hung in a gilt frame above the dining table. 'They said he died in action as a military hero,' she explained. 'But it was a lie. All lies.' She shook her head. 'He became intoxicated on plum schnapps and was eaten by a crocodile.'

'Is it true crocodiles store their food alive in their stomachs?' asked Feliks as they took their seats at the table.

There was a crash from outside: the shattering of crockery and the clatter of falling serving dishes and tureens. Suddenly Valentin appeared, fighting to restrain a small and unpleasant-looking man with round spectacles.

'Ostrovsky?' gasped Olga in obvious horror. 'What are you doing here?'

'Wouldn't you like to know?' said the man. 'I'll get you, Van Veenen,' he hissed. 'I'll repay you for the way you treated me. You mark my words.'

Olga rose from her seat. 'Valentin, kindly show this man to the door.'

The man leered unpleasantly as Valentin dragged him

from the dining room and ejected him from the Chop House.

'Who was that?' asked Greta, as Valentin returned with a silver tureen. He began ladling soup for Olga and the twins.

'That was Otto Ostrovsky,' whispered Olga. 'A most unsavoury character. A fellow author. He once claimed that I had stolen one of his ideas. Pure malice, of course, and not a word of truth in it. He vowed revenge, but as is the case with his books, his words are worth nothing.' She lifted the soup spoon to her mouth and was about to take a sip when Feliks cried out and snatched the spoon from Olga's hand.

Olga stared at the boy in surprise.

'Look!' said Feliks, reaching into the soup tureen with the ladle. Greta watched agog.

'Look at what?' asked Olga slowly.

'A death cap mushroom,' said Feliks, dredging up the offending fungus that floated on the surface of the soup.

Olga sniffed hard at the soup and turned to Valentin.

'He's quite right,' she said. 'The soup has been poisoned. Ostrovsky is trying to murder me.' She turned back to the twins. 'Tonight we will leave the city for Castle Van Veenen on the midnight express. It's not safe to remain in Schwartzgarten if Ostrovsky has turned to thoughts of murder. He may have agents and allies.'

'Just the soup,' murmured Valentin. 'He didn't have a chance to get his filthy claws on the other eatables.'

So the soup was removed from the table and Olga and the twins dined on white asparagus and poached salmon in mousseline sauce, as Valentin made preparations for their midnight departure.

CHAPTER FIFTEEN

That night they set out on their journey to Castle Van Veenen, wrapped in thick winter coats and fur hats. The twins were breathless with an intoxicating mixture of terror and excitement. It felt like moths exploding in their stomachs. Valentin drove them quickly through the silent streets in the Estler-Spitz to Schwartzgarten's Imperial Railway Station.

'It is vital that we do this,' Olga reassured the twins. 'We must get as far away from Ostrovsky as we can.'

Valentin unloaded the motor car as Olga led the twins through the first-class ticket office and out onto the platform. The tannoy crackled and hissed from high above them.

'The overnight express for Lake Brammerhaus will depart from platform eighteen.'

'But where is Karloff?' demanded Feliks, searching desperately for the bird.

'Karloff will remain in Schwartzgarten with friends,' replied Olga. 'It's safer for him here.'

The air was sharp with ice as the party were escorted to Olga Van Veenen's private carriage. The stewards had lined up along the platform, dressed in their distinctive red uniforms with gold braid.

'Good evening, Miss Van Veenen,' said a porter, tipping his hat.

Feliks watched as the provisions were loaded into the private carriage. There were wicker hampers filled with cakes and chocolates and crates of vintage champagne, as well as innumerable tins of dog food for Chou-Chou.

'This way,' said Olga, leading the twins onboard and through a tight wooden corridor into a small sitting room, sumptuously upholstered in purple velvet, and embroidered with intertwined serpents, the cipher of the Van Veenen family.

Valentin carried Olga's portable typewriter as the stewards hauled the remaining luggage onto the train. And finally came the cloisonné peacock, which Olga was never without.

'Valentin will take the motor car to Castle Van Veenen,' explained Olga. 'It is safer that we travel separately. Ostrovsky is more likely to follow a motor car than a steam train, and Valentin can lay a false trail.'

Valentin took his leave and Olga dropped her fur wrap onto a sofa as the pistons hissed. The guard blew his whistle and the steam engine pulled slowly from the platform and out through the Industrial District of the city.

The engine gathered speed, and Greta set off for the twins' cabin to unpack, leaving her brother alone with Olga. Feliks gazed out of the window as factory chimneys flashed by, relieved to be leaving Schwartzgarten behind and suddenly excited by the prospect of his journey to the north.

'You must be hungry, my little darling,' said Olga, patting Feliks gently on the head as he stared out into the darkness at the passing countryside. 'Do help yourself,' she purred, lifting the lid of a wooden box.

Feliks stared suspiciously inside. 'What is it?' he asked.

Olga laughed. 'Turkish delight, of course,' she said. 'Surely even an orphan knows Turkish delight when they see it?'

'But I don't like Turkish delight,' said Feliks.

'All little boys like Turkish delight,' insisted Olga,

squeezing a soft pink morsel of the rose-flavoured sweetmeat gently between her fingertips.

'I don't,' said Feliks. 'It makes me feel sick.'

Olga smiled indulgently, and popped the Turkish delight into her mouth. Chou-Chou yapped excitedly, and Olga tossed him a plump cube, which the Pekinese snapped down in a single, slavering bite.

Feliks went to join Greta in their cabin. He sat on his bunk and took out his pocketbook.

'I still don't trust her,' he said. 'Do you believe everything she says?'

'She's probably just the sort of person that dark things happen to,' pondered Greta. 'That's why people become writers in the first place.'

Feliks snorted.

'What are you writing?' asked Greta as her brother began to scribble a list in his book.

Feliks smiled. 'Things that Olga Van Veenen does that are strange,' he replied. 'I think it might be a long list.'

Greta sighed. It was clearly going to take a long time to

convince her brother how truly fortunate they were to have been taken in by a guardian as kind and generous as Olga Van Veenen.

They had a midnight supper in the dining car. It was a sumptuous meal of lamb cutlets and truffled eggs. The food was so delicious that Feliks stopped being suspicious until he had finished his dessert, an iced caramel mousse. After the meal, Olga sipped from a glass of champagne as the steward poured glasses of peppermint cordial for the twins. Olga dabbed her mouth with her napkin, leaving a bright stain of purple lipstick. She waited until the steward had left the carriage then lowered her voice conspiratorially.

'My darlings, we have to talk.' Greta and Feliks sat up straight. 'You must know, Ostrovsky is a dangerous and determined man. He will stop at nothing to carry out his plans.'

'But why is he trying to kill us?' asked Feliks.

'Some people are very jealous of talent,' said Olga. 'I have put you both in grave danger, my darlings. I could never forgive myself if anything terrible happened to you.'

Greta watched her guardian closely. There was something that Olga was not telling them.

'Haven't you informed the police?' asked Feliks, suddenly feeling sympathy for his guardian.

'The police?' laughed Olga. 'I telephoned the police before, but what did they do? Nothing.'

'Couldn't they arrest him?' asked Greta.

'He's too clever for the police,' moaned Olga. 'He thwarts them at every turn.'

The steward appeared at the table and coughed politely. He handed Olga Van Veenen a telegram, which she read in silence. At last, she placed the message on the table and stared forlornly out of the carriage window.

'What is it?' asked Greta. 'What does it say?'

Olga shook her head in despair. 'It's worse than I imagined,' she said.

She slid the telegram across the dining table to the twins.

Olga Van Veenen STOP Ostrovsky in pursuit STOP Advise extreme caution STOP Your life and lives of Mortenberg twins in grave danger STOP A friend.

When Greta and Feliks awoke the next morning, they could hear loud voices outside the window of their compartment. Greta climbed from her bunk and drew back the curtains. The train had stopped in a ravine.

Feliks sat up suddenly. 'What's happened?' he demanded. 'Is it an ambush?'

'I don't know,' said Greta. 'I can't see.' She pulled down the window and leant outside, calling to a porter who stood beside the carriage.

'What's happening, please?' she called.

'Avalanche, miss,' said the man, pointing to the front of the train.

The railway lines were blocked by a deep fall of snow, which had cascaded down into the ravine, and the driver and engineer were battling to clear the way. There were not enough spades to go round, so the stewards from the restaurant car were digging at the snow with polished silver trays.

After more than three hours of tireless digging, the iron snow plough was finally attached to the front of the steam engine. Enough of the snow and rock fall had been cleared from the tracks for the train to progress beyond the ravine. The pistons strained and the wheels sparked and slid on the rails.

There was a gentle knock at the door of the twins' cabin. 'Who is it?' whispered Greta.

'Porter, miss,' answered a voice.

Slowly, Greta opened the door and was relieved to discover that it was indeed a porter standing in the corridor, and not an assassin.

'Your guardian asked that you pack your suitcases as quickly as possible,' said the man. 'You'll be getting off at the next stop.'

Feliks packed their cases and ten minutes later the train ground slowly to a halt. Valentin stood patiently on a deserted railway platform, sheltering himself from the steady fall of snow beneath his familiar pinstriped umbrella.

'Any news?' asked Olga breathlessly, as the party made their way quickly from the train and out to the waiting motor car.

Valentin shook his head and remained silent.

Feliks and Greta climbed into the Estler-Spitz and Olga took her place beside them. She draped a reindeer skin around her shoulders and drew a fur over her legs. There were furs for the twins and an enormous box of caramel drops to fortify them on their journey to Castle Van Veenen.

As they drove, the snow became heavier, so Valentin was forced to stop the car and fix chains to the wheels.

'Make sure we're not followed,' said Olga, staring across the snow-covered track behind them. 'We don't know when Ostrovsky will attempt to strike next.'

The twins sat patiently inside the car, sucking caramel drops.

'Not much further now,' said Olga, as they set off once more and the motor car crawled through a dark pine forest, the turrets of a distant castle glimpsed fleetingly between the trees. They emerged from the forest into a small village, bouncing across the uneven cobbles. 'The village of Burg,' said Olga, as the twins gazed out of the windows.

There were a handful of thatched houses, and a scattering of tiny shops and taverns, behind which the walls of the castle loomed steeply. The chains on the wheels rattled and clanked over an ancient wooden bridge, connecting the village to Olga's ancestral home, and they came to a halt in front of the towering buttressed walls of Castle Van Veenen.

'We are expected,' said Olga as they climbed from the car and the studded oak door of the castle creaked slowly open.

A tall, lumpen woman stood in the shadows, reeking of stale cabbage.

'This is Helga, the housekeeper,' said Olga. 'Is dinner prepared?'

Helga shuffled forward, nodding her head.

'Excellent.' Olga smiled.

'Hello,' said Greta, holding out her hand. 'I'm Greta. And this is my brother, Feliks.'

Helga grunted.

'She doesn't speak,' said Olga. 'She can't or she doesn't. I don't remember which.'

Valentin unloaded the hampers and cases and carried them inside as the twins stared up at the soaring walls of the ancient castle.

'It has been in the Van Veenen family for generations,' said Olga. 'Many hundreds of years. I want you to explore,' she enthused. 'Discover every secret that the castle has ever held within its grey, stone walls.'

Greta and Feliks were to share a bedroom in the east wing, which looked out across the distant village of Burg and the snow-covered fields.

As soon as they had unpacked their cases, they set off to explore. There were countless corridors to negotiate which wound and twisted through the castle like the pathways of a maze. At the end of one particularly long passageway they discovered a doorway that had been concealed behind an ancient tapestry wall-hanging.

'This is exactly the sort of place where strange and mysterious things happen,' said Feliks darkly, turning the door handle and stepping through to a vast library with an eerily creaking wooden floor.

'I do hope so,' replied Greta with a smile and felt her pulse quickening.

———✦———

They dined at eight in the baronial hall. Olga was dressed in a long gown of pale green eau-de-Nil silk. Greta sat uncomfortably in her chair. Whenever she turned her head there was Helga, standing at the serving table, observing her every move. It was an unsettling feeling and Greta turned her head away.

The fire hissed and spat in the vast stone hearth. Valentin stood silently in attendance. From time to time he would throw a great log onto the fire, stoking it with an iron poker. Fir branches crackled as the amber sap oozed and dripped onto the smouldering embers.

After dinner, Olga sat back in her tapestry armchair beside the fire. She lifted the lid from a box of macaroons, and reached inside.

'What is this?' said Olga, withdrawing her hand from the box. She held between her fingers a small card, banded in black. 'The mark of Ostrovsky!' she gasped, pointing at an embossed letter 'O' in black ink, encirling the letter 's', which had been printed in red. 'Will you read it for me, Feliks?' she asked, her voice trembling.

Feliks took the card from his guardian and as he read his throat tightened.

Remember this, Olga Van Veenen. Tomorrow you all shall die.

CHAPTER SIXTEEN

Feliks woke early to find himself all alone in the vast, timber-beamed bedroom he shared with his sister. He climbed out of bed, and was making his way to the door when the handle turned slowly and he froze to the spot. Expecting Ostrovsky or one of his henchmen, he was relieved to discover that it was only Greta entering the room.

'They've gone,' said his sister, her eyes wide and her hands shaking. 'I knocked at Olga's bedroom door, but there's no one there. Her bed hasn't been slept in. I called for Valentin, but he didn't come. I think Ostrovsky has kidnapped them.'

Feliks dressed quickly and followed Greta out of the room.

'Hello?' called Greta, as they made their way along the landing. 'Is anyone there?'

Feliks held his hand over his sister's mouth. 'Wha—' mumbled Greta.

'Be quiet,' whispered Feliks. 'What if Ostrovsky is still here?'

'But the castle's silent,' protested Greta. 'Listen.'

They stopped and listened. Nothing could be heard, apart from the gentle creak of ancient timbers and the mournful howl of the wind outside.

'Maybe it's too quiet,' said Greta, and could feel her blood chilling at the thought.

Although the disappearance of Chou-Chou was hardly a reason for despair, the absence of Olga and Valentin was more disconcerting. The hall clock chimed the hour of eight as the twins crept silently through the deserted passageways of the castle.

'There's nobody here,' said Greta. 'We're all alone.'

'Maybe Ostrovsky broke into the castle in the middle of the night,' suggested Feliks.

'But why didn't he take us as well?' whispered Greta. 'He said he was going to murder us all.'

Hesitantly, they entered the silent expanse of the baronial hall. The embers had died in the grate and the room smelled of stale soot and wood smoke.

'I don't like it,' said Feliks, glancing around the empty hall, fearful that they were being watched. But it was only his imagination; they were quite alone.

Greta led Feliks out into the passageway, which ran the length of the castle, lined on either side with busts of Olga's ancestors. The Van Veenen family stretched back for generations, and some of the busts were hundreds of years old. At the far end of the hallway was a riveted oak door that led to the highest turret. Greta turned the iron handle.

'Do we have to go up so high?' asked Feliks. 'Why would Ostrovsky take Olga into the tower?'

'Maybe we can see tracks from up there,' said Greta. 'Some sign that Ostrovsky has been here.'

They climbed the turret's narrow stone steps, Greta first and Feliks trailing behind. The spiral staircase was steep, and the iron grips that once provided handholds were rusted or missing completely. Several times the twins slipped on the worn and uneven steps, before finally stumbling out through the stone doorway and onto the leaded roof at the very top of the turret. The tower was cloaked in mist, but by leaning carefully over the parapet, Greta was able to make out the snow-covered ground below, stretching off towards the distant village and the forest beyond.

'Don't lean so far,' said Feliks, gripping tightly to the door of the turret. 'If you get killed as well I'll be the only one left.'

There were no footprints leading from Castle Van Veenen, no tyre tracks and no sign that a sledge had pulled their unfortunate guardian away.

'Maybe there was more snow in the night?' said Greta. 'Then any tracks would be covered by now, wouldn't they?'

'I suppose so,' said Feliks. 'Maybe we should search the kitchen next,' he added hungrily, as his stomach growled and lurched.

Slowly, the twins descended the stone steps of the tower and made their way to the kitchens.

'Even Helga's gone,' said Greta, as they searched the pantry for supplies.

There were jars of anchovy and herring paste and pickled red cabbage from the Obervlatz Pickling Factory, enormous bottles of sausage and sauerkraut casserole, and crates and crates of nougat and Turkish delight. There was enough food to see them through the cruellest of winters, cut off from the outside world and far from Schwartzgarten.

'We can eat like princes,' said Feliks.

'Only if we live,' said Greta, whose mind was occupied with more pressing matters than a full stomach. 'If Ostrovsky has killed Olga, he'll have to kill us too. We know too much.'

But still, they had to eat.

As Feliks reached out towards a jar of hazelnut praline spread, his movements were arrested by a sudden gasp from his sister. She had lifted the lid off a box of pistachio nougat.

'Look,' said Greta, holding up a crumpled sheet of paper. 'A clue!'

'But there's nothing on it,' said Feliks.

Greta stared hard at the paper. In the bottom right-hand corner in tiny, spidery writing were the words: *decipher the old way*. And beneath these was the mark of Ostrovsky: the large 'O' in black, containing the letter 's' in red.

'What does he mean?' said Feliks. 'Decipher the old way?'

'Maybe it's written in invisible ink?' said Greta. She smiled. 'Remember what Mr Tantalus taught us?'

She took a match from a box on the shelf and lit it. Carefully, she held the paper above the flame. 'It's a map of the castle,' said Greta as a shape slowly began to appear on the paper.

'But why did Ostrovsky leave a map?' asked Feliks curiously. 'And why write "decipher the old way"?'

'I don't know,' said Greta. 'Even kidnappers make mistakes.'

Feliks frowned. 'But we don't even know that Olga has been kidnapped.'

'Then where is she?' demanded Greta.

This was a good point. There was no sign of their guardian, dead or alive. Greta pored over the map; it had now revealed its hidden secrets. The library was clearly marked, with an arrow pointing to a bookcase.

'Come on,' said Greta, running from the kitchen.

Feliks dropped the jar of praline spread into his pocket and followed his sister out.

At the bottom of the grand staircase they hurried past a statue of a peacock standing on a Grecian urn and continued on towards the Hall of Ancestors. Greta lifted the tapestry to one side and opened the door behind;

together the twins walked through to the library. Greta approached the bookcase that had been marked on the map.

'What are you looking for?' asked Feliks.

'I don't know,' answered Greta, scanning the spines of the books quickly in the hope of discovering another clue.

One book in particular seized Feliks's attention: *Recipes from the North-Eastern Region of the Country.*

'We haven't got time to think about food now,' said Greta, as Feliks pulled the book towards him.

There was a sudden grating of metal and the bookcase sank back into the wall and slid to one side, revealing a small stone chamber beyond.

Greta laughed, in spite of herself. It was as if one of Olga Van Veenen's adventure books had sprung magically to life. She took out the torch she carried in her pocket and directed the beam of light into the dark cavity.

'Come on,' said Greta, stepping into the chamber.

Feliks hesitated. 'But it might be dangerous.'

'Of course it's going to be dangerous,' replied Greta

with a smile. 'Secret passages always lead to dangerous places.'

This was not a reassuring thought, but nevertheless Feliks followed his sister into the dark stone chamber. A piece of paper lay crumpled on the floor and Greta stooped to pick it up.

'It's another map!' said Greta, holding the torch close. 'There's a passageway beneath here.' She traced her finger along the map. 'We need to go down. If we continue north, the passage runs the length of the castle.'

There was a staircase in the corner of the chamber, which wound down to an even smaller chamber below. A narrow passage led from this second chamber, so low that the twins had to bow their heads as they made their way deeper below the castle.

'We must be under the Hall of Ancestors now,' said Greta, pointing at the map.

The roof of the passageway became higher; the twins no longer had to stoop as they walked. But something was not quite right. They had reached a solid stone wall.

Greta stared at the map. 'It doesn't make sense,' she said. The battery was fading fast, but the pocket torch still threw out enough light to see by. 'According to the map there shouldn't be a wall here. The passageway should continue.'

'Look!' said Feliks suddenly. 'Another clue!'

A scrap of material had caught against an old iron bolt, the same colour as Olga's eau-de-Nil gown that she had worn at dinner the night before.

'It's from Olga's dress!' exclaimed Greta.

Feliks lifted the clue from the rusted bolt. As he did so, with a sickening screech of cogs and ratchets, a solid iron door lowered from the ceiling of the passageway behind them, blocking their path out. Greta pushed hard against the door, but it would not move. They were trapped.

'A stone wall in front of us,' said Feliks. 'And an iron door behind us. That's what the newspapers would describe as an unfortunate development.'

'It's Ostrovsky,' whispered Greta. 'He's lured us down here and now he's going to suffocate us.' She stopped and pressed her ear against the door. 'What's that noise?' she whispered.

'I didn't have breakfast, remember?' said Feliks irritably.

'No,' said Greta. 'Not that. Listen.'

From somewhere beyond the door could be heard the distinct gurgling of water.

'The tunnels are probably hundreds of years old,' said Feliks. 'It might be the sound of snow melting and dripping down through the rock.'

Greta turned. 'It's flooding,' she said, as a stream of water began to bubble up beneath her feet.

'We're going to drown,' said Feliks.

'I think that's the point,' replied Greta, as the stone chamber rapidly filled with ice-cold water.

'At least it will be quicker than suffocating,' observed Feliks, his teeth chattering from the cold.

The water quickly rose to waist height. Suddenly it seemed to ripple and surge towards them.

'It's like it's alive,' said Feliks.

Greta pointed the torch into the corner of the room to illuminate a stream of brown-backed cockroaches as they poured from a hole in the wall, spilling out into the icy water. Greta spluttered as the insects swarmed around her, scuttling up her arms and across her back. She flailed desperately.

'Help me!' she yelled. 'Do something!'

But Feliks did nothing to aid his sister; instead he watched the cockroaches with growing curiosity. 'Where are they going?' he asked.

Greta glared at her brother. 'How am I supposed to know?' she snapped.

Feliks shook his head. 'You don't understand. They've got to be going somewhere,' he said. 'We need to search.'

'What are we supposed to be searching for?' said Greta, shaking her arm to free half a dozen cockroaches which had wriggled up the sleeve of her pullover.

'If there's a way in, there's got to be a way out,' said Feliks. 'You said the wall wasn't marked on the map.'

He reached into the freezing water, running his hands across the uneven stone walls. Greta followed her brother's example and felt along the wall behind her. As she did so, her fingers sank into a groove between two stones.

'I think I've found something,' she cried, her hand grasping hold of an iron bar which had been embedded deep in the wall. 'I think it's a lever.'

'Pull it!' shouted Feliks.

'I'm trying!' answered Greta. 'It won't move.'

Water surged into the chamber and Greta lost her grip on the lever; she was swept up towards the rocky ceiling.

'I couldn't hold on,' she gasped.

'Don't speak,' said Feliks. 'We've got to save as much air as we can.'

'You have to to pull the lever,' said Greta. 'You're a better swimmer. It might be our only way out. Take this,' she said, passing Feliks the torch. 'It might just work underwater.'

Feliks took in a deep breath and ducked his head beneath the surface of the murky green water. The torch threw out a feeble light, but enough to find the iron lever in the stone wall below. He grasped it, just as the torch light blinked and faded, plunging the watery chamber into pitch-blackness. Feliks pushed his feet hard against the wall of the chamber to pull the lever forward and slowly it began to move. The stone wall receded into the ceiling and the twins were carried from the chamber on a tide of water, out into a narrow stone passageway beyond.

'I'm freezing,' said Feliks, as the water finally drained from his ears and gurgled out through a grate in the floor.

'We could have drowned,' panted Greta. 'At least we're still alive.'

'For now,' said Feliks.

His Brammerhaus tweed suit had absorbed so much water it had doubled in weight. He staggered through the passageway, soaked to the skin but gasping with relief. 'I smell of wet dog.'

The map, which Greta had been clutching in her hand, was a sodden mess. Feliks tapped the torch sharply against the wall and the bulb glowed dimly.

A large grey rat staggered along the passageway in front of them.

'We should follow him,' said Greta. 'He must know the way round the passageways better than we do.'

They followed the rat through a low doorway in the wall, scrambling on their hands and knees.

'I told you,' said Greta, 'he'll know the safest route.'

They found themselves in a small chamber with a low ceiling, arriving just in time to watch the rat being swallowed head first by a large black snake with bright yellow markings, which sucked in the rat's tail like a strand of spaghetti. Greta looked around to see more snakes writhing across the dusty floor. She felt the serpents coiling around her legs.

'Don't make them angry,' warned Feliks. 'They might be venomous.'

Greta's mouth was dry and her ears throbbed from the racing beat of her heart. She caught sight of a low opening at the opposite end of the chamber and carefully felt her way around the walls, all the time struggling to break free from the coiled snakes.

'Don't look down,' said Greta, squeezing Feliks's hand.

'Why would I want to look down?' said Feliks. 'I hate snakes.'

Greta stopped suddenly. 'And don't look up either,' she squealed.

Cogs and ratchets turned inside the walls. The ceiling was pressing down on them.

They lay on their stomachs to crawl through the opening as enormous spindle-legged spiders scuttled from the walls. Greta screamed and Feliks took her hand, pulling her forward with him. With a gasp of relief they emerged into a narrow tunnel as the ceiling of the chamber came crashing down behind them.

As Feliks struggled to regain his breath, Greta sniffed at the air.

'What is it?' whispered Feliks.

Greta sucked in a deep breath. The rich aroma of oil of petunia hung in the air and the dim flicker of a light could be seen at the end of the tunnel.

'It smells like her,' said Greta. 'Like Olga.' She took a step forward, but Feliks held her back.

'What if it's a trap?' he hissed.

Greta nodded and pressed herself tight against the tunnel's cold stone wall. Slowly and cautiously she made her way towards the light.

CHAPTER SEVENTEEN

The twins took care to look out for any booby traps that might have been laid to ensnare the unwary adventurer, but apart from a fat, moulting rat that dragged itself wheezing across the floor, the twins met with no further perils. The tunnel opened up into a large stone chamber, illuminated by the faltering light of an oil lantern. Sure enough, Olga lay bound and gagged on a narrow stone ledge.

'Is she still alive?' asked Feliks.

Greta nodded and quickly slipped the gag from Olga's mouth.

'Is that really you, my darlings?' said Olga weakly.

'We've come to rescue you,' said Greta.

There came a moan from the shadows.

'Who's there?' shouted Feliks.

'It's only Valentin,' said Olga, peering into the darkness. 'Poor, poor Valentin.'

Feliks picked up the lantern and held it in the direction of the moaning.

Valentin, who sat cowering in a corner, attempted to stagger to his feet.

'What's wrong with him?' whispered Greta.

Feliks took a step forward to help the man. 'I think he's been drugged,' he said.

'Don't be afraid, Valentin,' said Olga quietly. 'You're safe now.'

But this was not entirely true. Lantern light settled on the damp stone floor of the chamber, revealing Valentin's hand, lying at the man's feet, neatly severed at the wrist. The stump of his arm pumped blood in a steady stream, creating a sticky pool on the ground in front of him.

'His hand!' gasped Feliks.

'He tried to save me,' said Olga. 'See how they served him for his loyalty?'

'They cut off his hand?' whispered Greta.

'Don't look, my darling,' said Olga. 'It's too horrible.'

'Somebody should pick it up,' said Feliks. 'Maybe a doctor might be able to sew it back on again?' He reached towards the severed hand, but Valentin pushed Feliks roughly to one side. With his remaining hand he snatched up the dismembered one and dropped it into his jacket pocket. Pulling out a handkerchief, he pressed it hard against the stump, staunching the flow of blood.

'He needs to see a doctor,' insisted Greta.

'He'll be all right, won't you, Valentin?' replied Olga. Valentin grunted in the affirmative. 'You see?'

Greta untied the ropes at Olga's ankles and Feliks released his guardian's hands.

'My darlings,' gushed Olga, hugging the twins so tightly they could hardly breathe. 'However can I repay you?'

'But what about Valentin?' said Feliks. 'There must be a doctor in the village? If we can find a way out and pack the hand in ice, maybe it's not too late?'

'Don't you see?' whispered Olga. 'If we take him to a doctor, the truth will get out. That Ostrovsky has been unsuccessful in his plan to abduct and murder me. And who do you think he'll try to murder next?'

'Us?' gulped Greta.

Gravely, Olga nodded her head. 'He was going to leave me here to starve to death.'

'We'll all starve to death if we can't find a way out,' said Feliks. 'Then Ostrovsky will have succeeded.'

'How did you get down here?' asked Greta.

'I don't remember,' said Olga, holding her hand to her head. 'One moment I was sitting in my chair beside the fire, the next moment I woke up here.'

Valentin grunted and shrugged his shoulders.

'Ostrovsky must have drugged you both,' said Feliks.

'Very likely,' admitted Olga. 'I was eating macaroons. He must have laced the almond cream with a sleeping draught. Why, oh why was I so foolish? It was only luck that Helga wasn't here as well. She left late last night for her house in the village.'

'There must be a door or a hatch,' said Feliks, walking the circumference of the chamber. 'We can't get out the way we came.'

Greta picked up the lantern and walked towards her brother.

'No!' cried Feliks. 'Stay exactly where you are!'

'Whatever is the matter?' exclaimed Olga. 'Is it Ostrovsky? Has he come back to finish us off?'

Feliks dropped to his knees and scrabbled about in the dirt.

'Maybe he's not getting enough oxygen,' said Greta.

'He's gone strange in the head.'

'I haven't,' said Feliks firmly. 'Look. I didn't want you to disturb the footprints.'

Greta lowered the lantern. A distinct pair of footprints trailed the length of the cavern.

'What's so special about footprints?' asked Greta. 'It could have been Valentin.'

Feliks shook his head.

'Not Valentin,' he said. 'Valentin was only just waking up when we got here. He can't have walked anywhere. And look closely, these prints are much smaller than Valentin's.'

'So Ostrovsky left footprints,' said Greta, 'so what?'

'Look where they lead,' said Feliks, laughing. He took the lantern from Greta and held it high.

The footprints disappeared behind the stone ledge.

'But that's impossible,' said Greta.

'No, not impossible,' said Feliks. 'There must be another secret door here.'

'My clever boy.' Olga swung her legs from the ledge and climbed unsteadily to her feet. She reached out to support herself, leaning against a rusted iron hook. A dull grating sound could be heard from beyond the wall. 'What is that noise?' asked Olga.

Feliks reached up to the hook, but it would not move any further. 'Help me, Greta,' he said. 'Maybe if we both try.'

Greta climbed up onto the ledge, and pushed down on the iron hook as Feliks pulled. Finally, the hook began to move; and as it did so, the stone ledge slowly began to slip back into the wall of the chamber. Greta jumped down quickly, as another small room was revealed. Olga and Valentin watched in silence.

'There's a stone staircase,' said Feliks, straining his eyes in the cobwebbed gloom.

Valentin picked up the lantern with his remaining hand. He crossed the floor and stepped into the passageway.

'But what if it's a trap?' asked Greta. 'What if Ostrovsky is waiting at the top of the stairs to kill us?'

'What a delicious imagination you have,' said Olga with a smile. 'No, I think Ostrovsky is long gone. He abandoned us to our fate and has fled the castle and returned to Schwartzgarten. You can be quite sure of that.'

Slowly, Valentin led the way up the winding staircase.

Greta and Feliks followed behind, supporting Olga, who was still unsteady from the drugged macaroons.

At the top of the steps a wooden panel blocked their way. Valentin stopped and pressed his ear against it.

'Can you hear anything, Valentin?' whispered Olga.

He shook his head.

Feliks elbowed his way past the man and pressed his hand against the panel, which swung forward easily. They stepped out and found themselves once more in the library, at the opposite end of the room to the moving bookcase. Greta pushed the wooden panel closed behind her, blinking in the daylight though the sun was fast sinking beyond the castle.

'Safe,' whispered Olga.

But the twins were not so certain.

———•◆•———

As evening drew near, Valentin walked the halls and passageways of Castle Van Veenen, ensuring that all the windows and doors were secured against intruders. They dined early that night. Valentin served at table, and though he had lost a hand it did not seem to impede his movement in any way, nor did he show any apparent sign of pain.

'It's almost as though he never had another hand,' whispered Greta and Feliks nodded.

'A toast, I think,' said Olga suddenly, raising her glass. 'To my darling children, without whose bravery and ingenuity I should almost certainly have been left to rot beneath Castle Van Veenen.'

Greta and Feliks raised their glasses of lingonberry cordial.

'And now,' continued Olga. 'Now I shall write a book in honour of your adventures.'

CHAPTER EIGHTEEN

The nights had drawn in so it was almost pitch-black by three o'clock in the afternoon. Every day Olga Van Veenen typed, shut away in her study. For two weeks she wrote solidly; she typed five hundred words before breakfast, a thousand words before lunch, and another three thousand words before supper. She would appear briefly at mealtimes, staring distractedly at the twins as she took notes in shorthand in her leather-bound journal.

One morning, the twins woke early to the sound of the gong. Olga was standing in the hall to greet them as they descended the stone staircase.

'Good morning, my darlings,' she chirped, clutching the completed manuscript in her hands. 'At last, my book is finished. It is time to return to the city. I have been away from my public for too long.'

She clapped her hands and Valentin appeared from the kitchen.

'It is time to pack. Tomorrow we shall set off for

Schwartzgarten. Valentin, cable ahead to make sure my private carriage is prepared.'

<hr>

Greta and Feliks were relieved to return to Schwartzgarten, though they were still fearful of the threat posed by Ostrovsky. But as they sat with Olga in the shop of M. Kalvitas on their first afternoon back home in the city, drinking hot caramel chocolate, their guardian broke the good news.

'Ostrovsky is dead,' said Olga. 'I heard this very morning. The police found his body floating in the river beyond Schwartgarten. Our troubles are at an end.'

'And what about Karloff?' asked Feliks. 'Can we collect him today?'

But Olga shook her head. 'The bird escaped. You have Ostrovsky to thank for that.'

'I'm glad Ostrovsky is dead,' said Feliks, and Greta nodded sadly. A week after their return a parcel arrived, wrapped in brown paper and tied with string.

Olga beamed at the twins. 'The presentation copies of my new book!' she exclaimed in delight.

She placed the package on the hall table and untied the

string. She took out two copies of the book and handed one each to Greta and Feliks.

The books were bound in goatskin leather, and the edges of the pages were gilded. The title had been embossed in gold leaf:

Underground To Adventure.

The twins ran upstairs to their bedroom. Feliks placed his copy on his bedside table and turned instead to a new recipe he had been composing in his pocketbook. But Greta threw herself onto her bed and breathlessly turned the pages. Inside the cover was a printed dedication.

> *For Greta and Feliks, without whom*
> *this delightful adventure would not*
> *have been possible.*

Greta turned to a page at random and read:

> *Their beautiful guardian lay silently on the stone ledge. She had been bound and gagged.*
> *'Is she dead?' asked Johann, his heart pounding in his chest.*

Maria untied Miss Van Heffel's arms and gently
pulled the gag from her guardian's mouth.
'Is that really you, my darlings?' said Miss Van Heffel
weakly, as she slowly opened her eyes.
'We've come to rescue you,' said Maria.

Greta closed the book and frowned.

'What's wrong?' asked Feliks, looking up.

Silently, Greta passed the book to her brother. She sat watching as Feliks flicked through the book from beginning to end. After what seemed like an age he put it down and turned to face Greta.

'She hasn't changed a word,' said Feliks. 'Only our names. She's stolen our adventure. From the day she adopted us from the Reformatory to the day we rescued her in Castle Van Veenen.'

'She hasn't stolen anything,' said Greta defensively, snatching the book away from Feliks. 'All novelists have to get their ideas from somewhere.'

But Greta was unsettled. She spent the day reading the book and carried on reading late into the night.

Olga Van Veenen had promised to write a story in

honour of their adventure, but the novel was more fact than a work of fiction. And for reasons that Greta could not fathom, this troubled her greatly.

The following morning an invitation arrived by post.

'My darlings,' said Olga at breakfast, flourishing the gilt-edged invitation in her hand. 'The most exciting thing has happened.'

'Has the tiger escaped from the zoo again?' asked Greta.

'Even more exciting than that,' replied Olga. 'We've been invited to the Sunken City by the Guild of Booksellers.'

'On Lake Taneva?' said Greta suddenly.

Olga giggled and nodded.

'But it's days away by train, isn't it?' said Feliks.

'It would be if we were travelling by train,' laughed Olga. 'But we're travelling by airship, my darlings! By airship!'

That afternoon the twins were photographed for their passports, and were driven by Valentin with Olga to the aerodrome of the Schwartzgarten Airship Company several kilometres beyond the city walls. Feliks watched as Valentin steered the motor car with ease; on their return to the city, Olga had arranged for the man to be fitted with an articulated metal hand, which he now kept concealed inside a black leather glove.

'Look!' said Greta, as the enormous doors of the hangar slowly slid open, revealing the nose of the airship.

'This way, Miss Van Veenen,' said a steward, leading the party out onto the runway. They climbed the narrow aluminium staircase into the belly of the great silver airship.

The cases marked *NOT WANTED ON JOURNEY* were taken below to be stowed in the airship's vast hold.

'You could stow an elephant if you wanted to,' laughed the steward. 'Trouble is, nobody wants to.'

They were taken straight up to the promenade deck as Valentin carried the hand luggage on board.

'I've never been in an airship,' said Greta, gazing out at the runway below.

'Of course you haven't, my darling angel,' said Olga, stroking the side of Greta's face with her hand. 'You're an orphan. How could an orphan possibly afford to fly by airship?'

The passengers watched from the windows of the promenade deck as the airship inched out of the hangar.

A military band, dressed in scarlet uniforms, played an imperial march as the handling lines of the airship were released and the ballast water was emptied from the water tanks, soaking the band conductor who stood beneath. The engines spluttered into life and the airship suddenly began to rise like a child's balloon released into a windless sky. Feliks, who did not like heights, felt dizzy and sick – but it was a feeling that quickly passed.

It was growing dark. Greta peered down through the glass floor of the airship as it passed just inches above the pine trees of a vast forest, watching as nesting birds took wing, startled from sleep. She followed a road as it wound its way through the trees, passing over streams and rivers, before arriving at a far-flung village, where lights glowed faintly in the gloom and smoke curled upwards from the chimneys.

Feliks sat silently at a table on the promenade deck, his back to the window, and read from a book of recipes.

'So calm,' observed Olga. 'Nothing worries my brave little Feliks.'

That night, Greta lay in bed, avidly reading her guidebook to the Sunken City.

The walls of the cabin were paper-thin and the twins could hear Olga in the adjoining berth, as she tapped away at her portable typewriter.

'What if I get claustrophobic?' asked Feliks.

'You won't,' said Greta.

Feliks listened to the dull drone of the airship's engines. 'What if I get airsick, then?'

Greta snorted. 'There's a sink,' she said. 'Or you can lean out of the promenade window.'

Feliks opened a box of peppermint lozenges that he had packed for the flight, and climbed up into his bunk.

'The captain says we're flying at nearly eighty kilometres an hour,' said Greta. 'We arrive at the port late tomorrow afternoon and then we travel by steamer to the Sunken City. You'll hardly have time to feel claustrophobic or airsick.'

———◆———

They arrived at Lake Taneva the following day, an hour earlier than expected, helped along by a favourable wind. Mailbags and luggage were unloaded as the passengers disembarked. Olga, Valentin and the twins were collected by taxicab from the airship station and driven to a pavilion with a green copper roof on the northernmost shore of the lake. They boarded the steamer for the Sunken City, crossing the calm and icy waters as the sun sank low in the sky.

Olga stood on deck, clinging tightly to her hat as a breeze blew in from the distant Alps.

Valentin remained below deck with the luggage.

The lake is fed from the River Obe, read Greta. *Strictly speaking, the Sunken City is not an island at all. It is joined to the mainland by the most meagre tendril of land, beyond which an impassable mountain range rises steeply.*

Greta turned the page of her guidebook as the klaxon sounded, scaring away two white swans that had been flying close to the boat.

Olga ordered a pot of tea, which arrived on a flickering silver burner. She pincered an amber crystal of sugar with the tongs and dropped it into her cup.

'It's festival time in the Sunken City,' she observed, taking a small sip of her hot, sweet tea. 'So many wonders for you both to behold.'

They did not reach the Sunken City until nightfall,

when they stepped from the steamer and into a small boat, hardly larger than a canoe. A boatman rowed them through the canals of the city, which were illuminated by guttering torchlight as they passed beneath ornate marble bridges. Every now and then they caught sight of the grand plazas and imposing museums and galleries that Greta had read about in her guidebook.

'Excelsior Hotel,' said the boatman at last, pulling in his oars as the boat bumped gently against a flight of marble steps that had been carved into the wall of the canal. As he slipped the rope over a mooring pole, Greta and Feliks jumped out and Valentin helped Olga across to the steps. They climbed up to a small piazza, which led to the pink marble pillars at the entrance to the Excelsior Hotel. The piazza itself was festooned with garlands of bright paper lanterns. A doorman stood outside the hotel, dressed in a top hat and pink carnation buttonhole.

'Good evening, Miss Van Veenen,' said the man, removing his hat and bowing courteously to the visitors. 'It is an honour that you are staying with us once again.'

Olga smiled and swept past him into the lobby,

followed by the twins. Valentin carried in the cases from the boat.

The party had arrived late and the dining room was closed for the night, so supper was served in Olga Van Veenen's private sitting room. It was an elegantly decorated suite, with brocaded silk curtains and deep Persian rugs.

'I shall look after your passports,' said Olga, holding out her hands to the twins and taking charge of the documents. 'One can never be too careful in unfamiliar places.'

As Greta and Feliks sipped from bowls of steaming beetroot soup, Olga made quite certain that the passports were safely under lock and key.

'Why does she want our passports,' whispered Feliks. 'Is she keeping us prisoner here?'

It was the same thought that had passed through Greta's mind, but she slurped her soup and said nothing.

—◆—

Greta woke first the next day and pulled back the shutters. The room was flooded with pale morning light.

'Come and look, Feliks,' she said, stepping out onto the balcony and gazing at the city below.

It was beautiful. The architecture was very different to Schwartzgarten. Instead of slate-grey stone, the buildings were constructed of white sandstone and the pavements shone like polished marble.

'I'm hungry,' said Feliks as bells rang out across the city.

'All you ever think about is food,' said Greta.

There was a gentle knock at the door and Olga Van Veenen entered, a feather hat clinging to the side of her head.

'My darlings,' she said. 'I trust you both slept well?'

The twins nodded.

'Can you entertain yourselves this morning? I have to meet a publisher at the hotel. So tiresome. I would hate to deprive you of the chance to explore, before we meet at the bookshop this afternoon.'

———◆———

After breakfast the twins set off by boat. The water of the canals was cobalt blue in the sunlight. Pathways flanked the canals and bridges traversed the waterways. The boatman smiled at his young passengers and asked which route they wanted.

'Take us to the camera obscura, please,' said Greta.

'What is a camera obscura?' asked Feliks.

'It's like a telescope,' said Greta, reading from her guidebook. 'There's a hole in the roof of the building, and as the operator focuses the lens, images are projected on a screen in the centre of the room.'

The narrow tower which housed the famous camera obscura was reached by way of an ornate stone bridge, so wide that it spanned three of the canals.

'I wish there was an elevator,' panted Feliks as Greta ran ahead up the spiralling staircase.

'There are three hundred steps,' laughed Greta. 'I read that in my guidebook.' But even Greta was out of breath by the time they had reached the top of the tower.

As the operator focused the lens, Feliks suddenly pointed at the screen. 'Look,' he cried. 'It's Olga Van Veenen!'

Greta peered at the screen. Certainly the woman skulking along the back streets of the city resembled their guardian. 'But it can't be,' protested Greta. 'She said she would be staying at the hotel this morning to meet her publisher.'

'Her hat!' Feliks pointed at the screen. 'It's got to be her.'

The feathered hat clinging precariously to the side of the figure's head was identical to that which Olga Van Veenen had worn that morning.

'She's talking to somebody,' said Greta, staring hard at the screen as a second figure emerged cautiously from the shadows.

It was Otto Ostrovsky.

CHAPTER NINETEEN

I t had been decided that the twins would meet Olga at two o'clock in the afternoon outside the imposing Central Bookshop.

'It must have been a mistake,' said Greta, who had begun to question what she had witnessed in the camera obscura. 'It looked like Ostrovsky, but it can't have been. Ostrovsky is dead.'

'That's what Olga said,' replied Feliks. 'But where's the proof? We didn't see a body. We didn't read anything in the newspaper.'

Their guardian was already standing outside the bookshop, cloaked in a black velvet wrap beneath which she wore a voluminous dress of black taffeta embroidered with a thousand diamonds in the shape of the Van Veenen family cipher. Flags hung over the narrow streets to honour the arrival of the illustrious author. A group of children from the Van Veenen Adventure Society gazed in awe at her.

The bowed window of the antiquated bookshop was

carved with mythical and allegorical creatures. Inside the window, a perfect scale-replica of Castle Van Veenen had been shaped from neatly stacked copies of *An Adventure Underground*, beside which stood a life-size cardboard cut-out of the author.

'Delightful. Quite delightful,' laughed Olga, clapping her hands in approval. Catching sight of Greta and Feliks, she motioned for the crowd to part so the twins could approach. 'My darlings!' she cried.

Olga was photographed on the doorstep of the bookshop, clasping Greta and Feliks in a loving but suffocating embrace.

'Anything you want to say to your fans, Miss Van Veenen?' shouted a reporter from the crowd.

Olga held a hand to her heart. 'Sometimes people ask me what keeps me so young, and my answer is always the same.' A smile flashed across her face. 'Excitement.' She nodded. 'Yes, excitement and the companionship of children.' At this she reached out a hand to stroke Feliks's cheek and a photographer from *The Informant* snapped wildly. Feliks was almost blinded by the flashbulb.

The bookshop owner was a small, bald-headed and

sycophantic man, of a pale and sickly complexion, who gestured elaborately for Olga to enter his shop. The twins followed behind, gazing up at an enormous gingerbread castle decorated with elegant swirls of finely piped icing, which towered above them.

'Champagne,' demanded Olga. 'I must have champagne!'

'Of course, Miss Van Veenen,' said the bookshop owner, cowering.

An elegant pyramid of cut-glass champagne goblets was carried to the table. Olga inhaled two puffs of peppermint mouth spray and sat beside a mountain of neatly stacked books, sipping from a frothing glass of champagne. A line of children had gathered, clutching copies of her book in their eager hands. Olga smiled and a stream of purple ink flowed from the gold nib of her fountain pen as she inscribed the books for her adoring readers. The twins waited patiently, their suspicions growing with every passing moment.

'It was a good book,' said a snub-nosed girl in pigtails. 'I liked lots of bits.'

'But which bits did you like most?' asked Olga.

'I can't remember,' said the girl, suddenly alarmed by Olga's line of questioning.

'Remember something,' purred Olga with unwavering directness.

'But I can't,' said the girl blankly. 'I've forgotten.'

'Never mind,' replied Olga with a smile, though her teeth were gritted. She signed the book and pressed it into the girl's hands. *With love, Olga Van Veenen.*

It was three hours before the queue began to dwindle, and four hours before Olga instructed the bookshop owner to lock and bolt the door, drawing the blinds so the remaining children on the frozen pavement outside could not look in. Greta and Feliks exchanged anxious glances.

The bookseller, who had made a tidy fortune from the sale of Olga's books, wheeled out a tray of macaroons and delicate sponge cakes, topped with caramelised almond paste. The air was spiced with the scent of marzipan and toasted almonds, calling to mind Aunt Gisela's tragic demise, and the twins' tongues tingled with empathy and allergy.

The bookshop owner uncorked another bottle of champagne and refilled Olga's glass.

'And how have you been entertaining yourselves today?' inquired Olga, cutting into a soft lemon macaroon with her silver pastry fork. 'Have you been enjoying your time in the Sunken City?'

This was Greta's opportunity to question her guardian and she was anxious not to let the moment slip away.

'We visited the camera obscura,' she said. 'Do you know the camera obscura?'

This seemed to shake Olga; it was an answer and a question in the same breath, and this was unusual from her ward.

'Of course I know it,' replied Olga uncertainly, her eyes darting from twin to twin.

'It was strange,' said Feliks. 'We thought we saw someone we recognised.'

'Someone you recognised?' repeated Olga. 'How odd. So far from Schwartzgarten, in a city you have never visited before.'

'It looked like Ostrovsky,' said Greta defiantly.

'But it couldn't have been, my darlings,' said Olga,

cutting into a coffee macaroon with such force that her fork scraped with a tooth-numbing squeak against the porcelain plate. 'Because as I told you, the poor unfortunate Ostrovsky is quite, quite dead.'

Feliks was about to speak, but Greta kicked him under the table. There seemed little point in pursuing their line of questioning.

Olga smiled serenely. 'So you must have been mistaken, my darling angels.'

CHAPTER TWENTY

S lowly and cautiously, the twins entered Olga's
room. Their guardian was nowhere to be seen so it
seemed safe to explore. Drums and trumpets sounded as
the festival parade passed in the street below.

'What are we searching for?' asked Feliks.

'Some proof that Ostrovsky is still alive,' said Greta,
'and that he's in league with Olga.'

Suddenly, there were hushed voices in the corridor
outside. Searching desperately for a place to hide, Greta
seized her brother by the arm and dragged him into a
cupboard, pulling the door closed behind them.

Greta and Feliks hardly dared to breathe as Olga
entered the room, with Valentin following behind.

'If only some accident should befall them,' began Olga,
lost in thought.

'What sort of accident?' mumbled Valentin.

'The sort of accident that would prevent them opening
their darling cherub mouths ever again,' answered Olga.
She took a mouthful of aniseed mouthwash, threw back

her head to gargle the viscous concoction, and spat into the sink.

'Murder them here?' said Valentin doubtfully.

'Of course not here,' replied Olga, an explosive peal of laughter issuing forth from her painted purple lips. 'What a preposterous thing to suggest. Far too many witnesses.' She gazed at her reflection in the mirror and smiled reflectively. 'But then, of course, accidents do happen.'

Chou-Chou whined unpleasantly, scratching at the wardrobe door. 'What is it, precious darling?' asked Olga.

Olga turned the handle of the cupboard door and Greta and Feliks, tumbled out onto the floor.

'Eavesdroppers never hear good of themselves,' said Olga, staring down at the twins.

Greta and Feliks scrambled to their feet and backed towards the door.

Olga smiled. 'Not so quickly, my darlings,' she purred. 'Stay and talk with Auntie Olga.'

'You're not our aunt,' said Feliks.

'Have you heard everything?' asked Olga, fluttering her eyelashes impatiently.

'Everything,' said Greta.

'We know you want to murder us,' said Feliks.

'You're evil,' added Greta.

Olga shook her head. 'No, not evil,' she said, struggling to find the correct word. 'Misunderstood. I was the perfect mother to you both.'

'A perfect mother doesn't try to kill her children,' said Greta.

'I didn't want to kill you then,' said Olga, advancing slowly on the twins.

'But you want to kill us now,' protested Feliks.

Olga shook her head and pursed her lips.

'You haven't left me with any option, have you?' Her hand moved deftly across the writing desk and alighted on the cloisonné peacock. Her fingers closed slowly around the jewelled neck of the bird. 'You know you can never leave here.'

She lifted the peacock, revealing a stiletto blade, which had been concealed inside the bird's neck. It was a weapon the like of which the twins had never before seen; it had not one but two exquisitely sharp points, which glittered in the bright moonlight filtering in through the window. Greta and Feliks backed further towards the door, but Valentin was blocking their escape. He held up his umbrella and flicked a switch in the handle: with a quiet click, a spike emerged at the tip.

'Poisoned,' said Valentin. 'Just one scratch from this and you'll be dead in a minute.'

'We could have had all sorts of adventures together, but now,' Olga smiled, 'I think you're about to have a rather unfortunate accident.'

She raised the dagger high.

'What are you going to do?' stammered Greta.

'I think you know the answer,' said Olga with a smile, 'my little red-haired angel.'

'You'll never get away with it,' said Feliks.

'I gave you everything,' said Olga. 'You wanted for nothing. You had toys, pastries and adventures. Isn't that what every child wants?'

Suddenly, the door swung open, knocking Valentin off balance. A chambermaid entered carrying a bundle of freshly laundered towels.

'Run!' screamed Greta, seizing her opportunity to escape. She pulled Feliks with her and half-dragged him into the corridor, pushing past the maid's trolley and spilling fresh towels and bars of soap onto the floor.

'After them!' hissed Olga. 'Don't let them get away!'

Valentin hurried out into the hall, followed by Chou-Chou, who yapped excitedly.

'Don't slow down,' screamed Greta, pulling Feliks along behind her.

The elevator bell rang. The doors slid open and a small woman stepped out, struggling to control a large black poodle.

'Quickly!' shouted Greta, skidding to a halt inside the elevator. 'Press the button!'

Feliks pressed the button but the elevator doors did not close.

'He's coming,' gasped Greta, as Valentin ran towards them, attempting to dodge the fallen towels and soap. He stumbled against the black poodle, which snapped at his legs, tearing a hole in his trousers. Chou-Chou fled in panic as the poodle pursued him into the suite, almost knocking Olga to the floor.

'Press the button!' yelped Greta. 'Press it again!'

Feliks hammered his fist against the button and the doors slowly began to move.

Valentin made a desperate grab, and in doing so slipped on a bar of soap and lost his balance completely.

The doors slid shut and the elevator lurched downwards to the lobby.

The twins ran across the polished marble floor, skidding though the revolving door and out onto the street.

'A letter for you,' called the reception clerk, running after the twins and handing Feliks an envelope.

'Please don't tell Miss Van Veenen where we've gone,' Greta shouted back, as the clerk returned to the hotel. 'She's trying to murder us.'

'Where do we go now?' panted Feliks, slipping the envelope inside his pocket. There was no time to stop and read the message.

Greta pointed ahead of her. 'We need to get a boat back to the mainland.'

The festival crowds were parading through the streets of the Sunken City, carrying decorated banners. The music was deafening as Greta and Feliks negotiated their way. Greta glanced back and saw a figure fighting through the crowds.

'Look,' said Greta. 'It's Valentin!'

The twins doubled back and crossed to the other side of the festival parade. Valentin pushed through the throngs of festival-goers, unaware that the twins had changed direction.

'It's working,' said Greta. 'He's gone the other way.'

'What do we do now?' asked Feliks, as they stepped back into the shadows of a narrow alleyway.

Greta leant against the wall to think. 'We've got to get far away from here,' she said.

They followed the alley to a small and silent piazza bordering a canal. The water glowed like a river of fire in the guttering lamplight. Feliks stopped and strained to listen to a far-off noise.

'What can you hear?' whispered Greta.

It was the distant but distinct hum of an outboard motor, and the metallic clang of a police bell.

'It's the police,' said Feliks. 'They're coming for us!'

Greta took her brother by the arm and they pressed themselves tightly against the wall. But as they made their way slowly back to the main street, creeping through the shadows, they could see that two customs officials were erecting a wooden barrier, painted with the words: *PASSPORT CONTROL*.

Greta felt in her pocket.

'What is it?' whispered Feliks.

'Our passports,' said Greta. 'Olga still has them in her safe.' The reality of their precarious situation struck her forcibly. 'We're trapped here.'

'What do we do now?' asked Feliks.

Greta did not have an idea in her head. They could not continue along the alley to the passport control. Without their passports they would surely be returned to Olga and inevitable death.

'This way,' she whispered. 'Back to the piazza. But watch out for Valentin and the police.'

They walked the few steps towards the deserted square. They could go no further by foot; the canal barred their way. Greta stared around her, hoping for inspiration to strike. Up above, in the top storey of a deserted shipping agency, torchlight could be glimpsed through the frost-covered windows.

'The police are getting closer,' whispered Greta. 'I'm sure they're up in that building looking for us now.'

They stood back beneath an archway as the beam of one of the torches flashed down from a window and onto the canal below, illuminating a moored barge covered with an oilskin sheet.

'There,' said Feliks, pointing to the barge. 'We can hide under the oilskin until the police have gone.'

'That's a stupid idea,' said Greta, wishing she had thought of it herself.

'Have you got a better one?' demanded Feliks.

But of course Greta did not. They waited patiently until the torchlight moved from the window, and then ran silently across the paving stones of the piazza. Feliks lifted the oilskin as Greta ducked underneath, and then followed his sister onto the boat, fastening the cover behind him.

There was not much room in the hold of the barge, crammed to the gunnels as it was with crate after crate of spiced gingerbread.

'At least we won't starve,' said Feliks optimistically.

'It might be the last meal we ever eat,' replied Greta, suddenly overcome by a morbid sense of their unhappy predicament. Her mood did not lift as she heard footsteps nearby, echoing sharply around the enclosed courtyard.

'Police?' murmured Feliks.

'Or Valentin?' said Greta.

The stranger climbed up from the piazza and walked slowly around the deck of the barge. Feliks held on to Greta tightly, hardly daring to breathe.

The footsteps passed to the back of the boat and a hoarse voice cried out:

'Damn you! Curse the lot of you! The finest gingerbread to pass the lips of princes! Well, I'll be gone and there's an end to it.'

There was more angry muttering, followed by a rattle and roar from the outboard motor which sent violent tremors along the length of the barge. Greta peered out from beneath the oilskin; the boat was passing slowly along the canal and out towards the open waters of Lake Taneva. A parting oath was screamed from the back of the boat:

'May the next piece of gingerbread you eat choke the very life from you!'

Greta crawled back towards her brother.

'Where are we going?' asked Feliks.

Greta shook her head. 'I don't know. I think we're

heading back to the port at the other side of the lake. We'll wait until the captain of the barge is long gone and then we'll try to see if we can hide away on a train to Burg.'

'To Burg?' spluttered Feliks.

'We have to get back to Castle Van Veenen,' whispered Greta.

Feliks stared at his sister in disbelief. 'Isn't that the first place Olga would look for us?'

'But why would she?' replied Greta. 'She'd expect us to go into hiding. We have to go to Burg, Feliks. We need to find evidence.'

Suddenly, the oilskin was ripped back, revealing the night sky above. An elderly man with a grey moustache and a blue cap loomed over them.

'Stowaways, eh?' whispered the man with grim satisfaction. 'Espionage and skulduggery! I can't wait to see the look on your faces when she cuts out your black little hearts.'

A bell sounded across the water and he stopped and turned.

'We're looking for two children,' shouted a police officer from a motor launch. 'Twins.'

'Is that a fact?' said the old man, dropping the oilskin back into place. 'Well, I haven't seen any. Not a sight or sign of twins in your whole cursed city.'

The boat motored away, and once more the old man pulled back the oilskin.

'Now where was I?' he asked.

'You said you couldn't wait until Olga cut out our black little hearts,' said Greta.

'Olga?' said the old man. 'Olga who?'

'Olga Van Veenen,' said Feliks. 'She writes adventure books.'

'Don't go in for adventure-book reading as a rule,' said the old man. 'Storybooks knock out all the thoughts a man has stored away in his brains. And when you get to my great age, it isn't worth the risk. Books on battles and bloodshed, that's a different matter altogether. Can't get my fill of battles and bloodshed.'

'If you're not working for Olga Van Veenen,' said Greta, 'who exactly is it that wants to cut out our black little hearts?'

It seemed unfortunate indeed if another enemy had designs to eradicate the Woebegone Twins.

'Her,' said the old man, tapping his finger against one of the crates of gingerbread. 'Mrs Brandelbrot.'

'Brandel-who?' asked Feliks.

'BRANDELBROT!' screamed the old man, shaking his fists in frustration. 'Brandelbrot's Spiced Gingerbread!' He sat down on the crate and moaned miserably.

'But we've never even met Mrs Brandelbrot,' said Greta. 'So why does she want to kill us?'

The old man stared at her. 'Gingerbread theft,' he said. 'Eats into her profits, it does, gingerbread theft.'

'But we haven't stolen any gingerbread,' said Feliks.

'So why were you hiding in the barge?' asked the old man.

'We're escaping from someone,' said Greta.

'Why didn't you say so before?' said the man. He stood up and laughed. 'That puts a different complexion on things. So what is it you've done?' he asked with a wicked gleam in his eye. 'Murders, is it?'

'We haven't murdered anyone,' Greta scowled. 'But if we'd stayed in the Sunken City we would have been corpses by the morning.'

'Well, we can't have that, can we?' said the old man.

He gazed out across the lake. 'We're off course,' he said. 'If I don't put us right, we'll end up back where we started.' With his hand on the tiller he steered the boat in the direction of the port.

The old man, whose name was Kirtzman, explained to the twins that he was a commercial traveller for Mrs Brandelbrot's Spiced Gingerbread and had travelled to the Sunken City for the festival.

'Didn't sell one crate,' he said bitterly. 'Not one single, sorry crate.'

'Is it good gingerbread?' asked Feliks.

'No, it is not,' said Kirtzman. 'I wouldn't give it to my wife if her life depended on it. Battles and bloodshed, that's what I longed for. Bravery, battles and bloodshed, not spiced gingerbread. But we have our lot in this life and we make the best of it.'

They were fast approaching the port, and the old man instructed the twins to hide themselves away again until he was certain that there was no sign of the police. Soon Kirtzman gave a low whistle, and the twins re-emerged and stood up on deck as the boat drew alongside the harbour wall.

The old man secured the boat to an iron ring. He lit a lantern and held it high as Greta and Feliks jumped from the boat. Together, they carried the crates of gingerbread towards Kirtzman's motor van, which he had parked beside an empty warehouse.

'Where are you headed next?' he asked as he slid the last of the crates into the van and swung the door shut.

'To Burg,' said Greta.

'And that's a coincidence,' said the old man, 'because that's precisely the place I'm heading for.' He was not – but as he was travelling close to the village and had taken pity on the twins he had decided to change his route accordingly.

'Do many people buy gingerbread in Burg?' asked Feliks. 'Olga Van Veenen has her castle there. It's an evil place.'

'That may be,' said the old man, his face cracking into a snaggle-toothed grin. 'Wherever a heart is blackest, that's where a man in my line of work finds the tooth is sweetest.'

They jumped up into the motor van and Kirtzman started the engine. He passed Greta a bottle of smelling salts. 'You seem like a sensible girl,' he said. 'If I fall asleep at the wheel, you unscrew that bottle and hold it up under my nose. The smell will bring me round again.'

This was not a comforting thought, so Greta gripped the bottle tightly in her hand in case of emergency. And emergencies frequently occurred. Whenever their travelling companion began to weave across the road, Greta would unscrew the lid of the smelling salts and waft the bottle under Kirtzman's nose as instructed. With a snort, the man would return to his senses, carrying on his conversation exactly where he had left off.

'...did I ever tell you what I craved most in this life?'

'Bravery, battles and bloodshed?' asked Feliks.

The man chuckled and nodded. 'I could run a man through with a sword, that's for certain. Till the blood spurted out in torrents.' And with that he slumped over the steering wheel again, snoring loudly.

＊

At dawn they stopped at the roadside and the old man made up a fire of fallen twigs and rotten branches and boiled a kettle with water from a stream. He sprinkled powdered ginger in a bowl of hot water and soaked his feet, as the twins sat and ate the wretched spiced gingerbread, which was even more unpleasant than Kirtzman had admitted; it was as dry as cardboard and tasted strongly of mildew. And as they sat and talked in the pale morning light, matters turned to the twins' journey to the village of Burg and Castle Van Veenen, and Olga's attempts to murder them.

'I can't stand by and let murderings happen,' declared Kirtzman, as snow began to fall. 'Consider me your loyal comrade-in-arms. Maybe Fate's finally given me my moment for battles and bloodshed!'

But as they continued their journey the motor van began to slide on the icy road. The engine steamed and they came to a spluttering halt.

'I can't go any further,' said the old man, shaking his head. 'The engine's dead.'

'Can we help you mend it?' asked Greta.

'It's beyond that,' said Kirtzman. 'You'll have to go on alone.'

The twins climbed down reluctantly onto the frozen road. The snow was falling heavily.

'Which way is it?' asked Feliks.

'That way,' said the old man, pointing towards the distant forest. 'Through the trees and beyond. That will take you to Burg.'

'And what will you do?' asked Greta.

'I'll have to stay here with the motor van,' said Kirtzman. 'Mrs Brandelbrot would have my liver for breakfast if I abandoned this gingerbread here. It's a pity too, because I had a hankering for battles and bloodshed.'

And so the twins said their goodbyes and set off across the snow. The old man waited until the twins were out of hearing, then he started the engine and drove away with a heavy heart.

His days of battles and bloodshed were far behind him.

CHAPTER TWENTY-ONE

O nce more the Woebegone Twins were all alone. They were not dressed for the cold, and they shivered in the icy air.

'Keep your head down,' said Greta as they finally emerged through the trees and arrived at the outskirts of Burg. 'In case anybody recognises us.'

But the street was deserted. A spindly plume of smoke rose from the chimney of the tavern at the edge of the village, but that was the only sign of life. The houses were shuttered against the snow.

They made their way cautiously across the bridge towards the towering turrets of Castle Van Veenen. Somehow, it appeared even more sinister and foreboding than before.

'It's because we know the truth now,' said Greta thoughtfully, as they trudged on through the snow.

'I told you,' said Feliks as they approached the walls of the castle. 'Good things only ever happen in books. Not in real life.'

Greta tried the door but it was locked. Peering through a

window, the furniture was covered in dust sheets.

'There's nobody there,' said Feliks.

'Exactly,' said Greta. 'Olga won't come here. She'll travel back to Schwartzgarten, and look for us there.'

'What about Helga?' asked Feliks.

'She'll be safe in her house in the village,' replied Greta. 'Why would she be at Castle Van Veenen if Olga isn't?'

After searching for some time, Feliks discovered that a window to the kitchen had been left ajar, and by levering it open with a fallen branch he was able to create enough of a gap to wriggle inside. Greta followed behind. They dropped noiselessly onto the top of a cupboard and climbed down the shelves like the rungs of a ladder.

'We should get supplies,' said Feliks. 'We can't stay here, but we do have to eat.'

'That's stealing,' replied Greta, imagining what Aunt Gisela would say.

'But we'd be stealing from Olga,' said Feliks. 'So she'd deserve it.'

Greta agreed, and they filled Feliks's satchel with jars of food from the castle's stores.

They crept from the kitchens and up the stone staircase

that led to the Hall of Ancestors.

'We need to go back to the library,' whispered Greta. 'There must be evidence against Olga somewhere in the castle.'

'Why do we need evidence?' asked Feliks. 'We'll just tell people what happened.'

'We're children,' said Greta, rolling her eyes ironically. 'Nobody ever believes what children say.'

Feliks lifted a carved wooden sword from a brass hook on the wall and held it aloft for protection. As they passed the great staircase he was startled by a creak from an ancient floorboard.

'Who is that?' demanded Feliks. 'Show yourself!' He swiped at the air with the blade of the woodworm-riddled sword, which crumbled in his hands in a cloud of golden dust. Greta stumbled against the ornate peacock at the foot of the stairs. To stop herself from falling, she clutched at the peacock's head. And as she did so it swivelled backwards, revealing a brass switch beneath.

'Have you broken it?' said Feliks. 'She'll know we've been here.'

'It isn't broken,' said Greta, inspecting the switch

closely. 'It was hiding a switch.'

'Don't press it,' said Feliks. 'We don't know what it—'

The words died on his lips. Greta had already pressed the switch. A section of the panelled wall, bearing the crest of the Van Veenen family, slid back into the brickwork.

'Another secret room,' said Greta. She was fast growing sick of secret rooms and concealed passageways.

But the chamber was different to those the twins had explored far beneath the castle.

'It looks new,' said Feliks.

There was a coat hook on the brick wall and a half-eaten dog biscuit on the floor. There was even an electric bulb in the ceiling to light their way, as they followed a winding iron staircase down into the very bowels of the castle.

Passing a dusty wine cellar, they came to the door of another room. The large brass handle turned easily. Here, the walls were made from wood; all except the opposite wall, which was made of plaster.

A movie camera marked *Von Merhart Movie Corporation*, was mounted on a tripod, pointing through a hole in the plaster wall.

Greta placed her eye against the viewfinder. She pulled

her head back and stared at Feliks in bewilderment.

'What is it?' asked Feliks gently. 'What have you seen?' He put his eye to the movie camera and found that he was peering through to a stone chamber beyond. It was the same chamber they had almost drowned in, with the iron door and the secret lever.

'She was filming us,' said Greta quietly. Feliks stared up at a high shelf, neatly piled with cans of movie film, each carefully labelled.

'Friedrich and Lottie. Tatiana. Bertolt,' read Feliks. 'A lot of children came and went before Olga took us from the Reformatory.'

Greta nodded. She pressed a switch on the plaster wall. As she peered through the viewfinder once again she could see that a stone had receded in the chamber, releasing a swarm of brown-backed cockroaches.

Feliks suddenly clutched at Greta's arm. He held out a photograph of Olga standing at the entrance to Castle Van Veenen, which had been taken many years before the twins had met her.

'It's Olga,' said Greta. 'It's not important. We need to find evidence.'

'But this is evidence,' said Feliks. 'There. See?' He pointed at another figure in the photograph. It was Valentin, dressed in his chauffeur's uniform. Feliks pointed at Valentin's left arm and Greta stared in disbelief at the photograph. There was nothing more than a stump where Valentin's hand should have been.

'He never had a left hand,' said Greta at last.

'Well, it didn't grow back, did it?' said Feliks sarcastically. It was difficult for Greta to take this in.

'It must have been an artificial hand,' she said.

Feliks considered this. 'Yes,' he said with a smile. 'That's why Olga didn't want us to get too close to him. Because we'd find out the truth. That it wasn't a real hand.'

'But it looked so real,' said Greta.

Feliks opened the drawers of a filing cabinet that stood in the corner of the room, reached in and took out a large roll of paper.

'What is it?' asked Greta impatiently as Feliks slowly unrolled the paper.

'Maybe it's a map.'

It was not a map, but blueprints for the underground chambers, intricately drawn and signed: *Fritz Von Merhart*.

'They're not ancient catacombs at all,' said Greta. 'It's like a movie set.'

'Nothing is real,' said Feliks, recalling Aunt Gisela's words, 'but everything looks real. This was all designed by Von Merhart.'

'Perhaps that's why he was killed?' said Greta. 'Because he knew too much?

'Maybe he was blackmailing her,' said Feliks, continuing to hunt through the filing cabinet. He pulled out a letter.

'Here,' he said, 'Brandberg Brothers. It's a receipt from the construction firm that was burned to the ground in Schwartzgarten. Another motive for murder. Do you think Olga tried to dispose of everybody that knew of these underground chambers?'

Greta pushed Feliks to one side. A battered cardboard box at the bottom of the drawer had caught her eye. She reached in to retrieve it and lifted the lid. Inside the box lay Valentin's hand, carved from wax and painted to resemble the pallid colour of his own skin. Alongside the hand was a pump to dispense artificial blood, still smeared a syrupy red.

Greta opened the door to the next room. Like the room she had just left, a movie camera pointed out into the chamber beyond. A wooden crate on a shelf was marked: *Brown-Backed Cockroaches*. Greta shivered.

'Look!' said Feliks.

Greta turned. Feliks had opened a cupboard. The shelves were crammed full of every make of perfume and eau de toilette under the sun. On the bottom shelf was a half-used bottle of oil of petunia.

'So she doesn't even like oil of petunia,' said Greta. 'That was a lie as well. She was only using it to remind us of Aunt Gisela.'

Feliks was busily collecting tins of film.

'We should go,' said Greta. 'Somebody might come back to the castle.'

Feliks picked up an empty box and stowed the evidence safely inside.

Together they made their way back out of the catacombs and into the dark and shuttered library.

There was a loud creak at the far end of the room. Greta gasped and Feliks felt his blood run cold.

Slowly, very slowly, a large figure shuffled through the gloom towards them, a meat cleaver raised high above its head.

CHAPTER TWENTY-TWO

The cleaver glinted in a beam of pale sunlight that filtered through the shuttered windows. The figure approached them slowly across the library floor. The lives of the Woebegone Twins were shortly to come to a sticky end, of that Greta was quite certain.

Feliks's initial fear was tempered by a reassuringly familiar smell of stale cabbage.

'Helga?' he whispered. 'Is that you?'

The figure shuffled backwards and grunted in the darkness. Greta switched on her pocket torch and Helga flinched, shielding her eyes from the bright light.

Greta was not entirely sure whether the sight of Helga was cause for relief or alarm. After all, she was housekeeper to Olga Van Veenen.

'It's very good to see you again,' said Feliks, fighting hard to put on a brave face.

Helga stared down at him. Her dark eyes had a haunted expression. Rather than proceed to slice the boy into slivers as Greta was grimly expecting, Helga wiped tears from her eyes with the backs of her hands and scooped up the twins in a fond embrace, almost lifting them from the ground with her enormous strength.

But still not a word tumbled from the lips of the housekeeper. Nor did she relinquish her grip on the meat cleaver, as she led the twins out of the castle and over the snow-covered landscape.

'Why did we have to leave so quickly?' asked Greta.

'Do you think Olga might return?' said Feliks suddenly.

Helga grunted and nodded. She hurried onwards and the twins battled to keep up. The temperature had dropped, and a fresh snowfall made the journey more arduous than before.

Feliks, still carrying the box of evidence, turned back to gaze once more at the grey and forbidding castle walls.

But Helga grunted and beckoned him on. She led them over the ancient wooden bridge that forded the river and along the village street, past the shuttered shops and houses. She stopped outside a narrow stone building with a thatched roof and hammered at the door.

'Who is it?' came a voice.

Helga grunted.

'Helga?' said the voice.

The door creaked open and a bearded face peered out cautiously. Helga pushed her way inside, pulling the twins with her.

The bearded man locked and bolted the door behind them. 'What have you done?' he asked, turning to Helga and looking down at the twins. 'Why have you brought them here?'

The twins stood shivering.

Helga grunted again and smiled at the man. He nodded and smiled back.

'I am Helga's husband, Ulrich,' said the man at last. 'I expect you're both hungry?'

'We haven't eaten anything since yesterday,' replied Feliks mournfully. 'Apart from a bar of nougat. And some gingerbread.'

'There's food on the stove,' said the man. 'We need to take the chill out of your bones.'

Helga smiled, and served up two steaming bowls of potato pasta, topped with crisply fried onions and a large dollop of apple sauce. The twins sat beside the blazing fire, grateful for the warmth and nourishment.

Ulrich shook his head and sighed.

'Castle Van Veenen's been standing for five hundred years and nothing good has happened inside its walls in centuries,' he said.

The twins pulled their stools closer to the fire. Ulrich sharpened the blade of an axe as he talked, stopping at regular intervals to take large gulps of rye beer from a pewter tankard.

'You're not the first children Olga Van Veenen's taken to that cursed place,' he said.

'We know there were others,' said Greta.

Helga nodded, her eyes fearful and unblinking.

'Oh, yes,' whispered the man. 'There were others.' He leant forward in his chair. 'And what's become of them, nobody knows.'

Helga hung her head and uttered a quiet moan.

'But we hold our tongues,' said Ulrich, 'Helga, because she can't speak a word, and me...well,' he put down the axe and ran his fingers through his beard. 'Because I'm a coward, I suppose. And if I did say anything, then Helga and me, we'd be the very next ones to disappear. You mark my words.'

Feliks shuddered and Greta gasped as Ulrich slowly drew his finger across his throat.

———•———

It was pitch-dark outside as Ulrich spirited the twins from the house.

'It's not safe to stay here a minute longer,' he whispered. 'Van Veenen has spies everywhere.'

The snow had settled and frozen as they walked through the silent village and out across the fields, wrapped in blankets that Helga had pinned around their shoulders.

'There's a railway halt not far,' said Ulrich. 'The midnight express passes through on its way to Schwartzgarten. It's only a small place, but the train still stops. It runs through the grounds of another castle, the home of Baron Maxim. He pays the Imperial Railway Company so much every month to stop outside his castle. Some nights he catches the express, some nights he doesn't. It's all the same to him. You can travel to Schwartzgarten and no one will be any the wiser.'

They waited at the silent railway halt for over an hour. Helga's husband refused to leave the twins until the train had arrived, which it did shortly after midnight. A porter stepped off onto the frozen platform.

'Baron Maxim?' he called.

'That's right,' Ulrich called back. 'Baron Maxim's grandchildren. They are travelling to Schwartzgarten.'

The porter opened a door to a private compartment and Greta and Feliks stepped aboard. They opened the window and thanked Ulrich for his help and he stood to wave them off before trudging back across the vast, snow-covered fields to Burg.

'Hot chocolate?' asked the porter as the twins settled back in their seats in the warm and comfortable compartment. 'Your grandfather always has his with cinnamon and whipped cream.'

It seemed impolite to refuse, so the twins sipped from frothing mugs of steaming chocolate as the train thundered along the tracks. Feliks rummaged through the box of evidence and made an inventory of the clues they had collected, which he wrote neatly in his pocketbook. When he had finally finished he sighed, deep in thought.

'It was like a complicated magic trick,' said Feliks at last. 'We saw exactly what Olga wanted us to see.'

He slipped the book back inside his overcoat pocket and pulled out a lump of nougat. Stuck to the wrapper was a small envelope, addressed: *The Mortenberg Twins, Excelsior Hotel.*

'What's that?' asked Greta sitting up in her seat. 'It's addressed to us.'

'From the hotel in the Sunken City,' said Feliks, suddenly remembering. 'When we were escaping from Valentin. I forgot I still had it.'

He tore open the envelope and slipped out a small, neatly folded railway timetable.

'Is there a note?' asked Greta.

Feliks looked inside the envelope, but there was nothing else to find. 'It's just the railway timetable.'

'No,' said Greta, taking the timetable from Feliks. 'Look there.' She pointed at the paper. A single station had been underlined in red ink: *Stoller.* 'Perhaps it's a trap. Perhaps somebody want to lure us to the place to murder us?'

'It's only Olga that wants to murder us,' said Feliks. 'As far as we know, anyway. I think it must be a friend. Somebody who wanted to help us escape from Olga's clutches.'

Greta rang the service bell and the Porter appeared.

'More hot chocolate?'

Feliks shook his head. 'Does the express stop at Stoller?' he asked.

'We go through it but we don't stop,' replied the porter. 'Nothing there to stop for.'

'But *could* the train stop there?' persisted Greta.

'For the grandchildren of Baron Maxim, the express could stop anywhere,' said the porter with a smile.

It wasn't until eight o'clock the following morning that the express pulled into Stoller station. The train was so long that the driver had to stop many yards beyond the station so that the twins could step from their carriage and alight on the platform.

'I thought there'd be someone here to meet us,' said Greta as the express train gathered speed and disappeared into the distance.

'How would they know which train we'd catch?' asked Feliks.

Greta nodded, but was nevertheless disappointed to find the station empty.

The sign to the Stationmaster's office creaked and

groaned as it swung in the breeze.

'I don't like it here,' said Feliks, pulling the last curselings from his pocket and inserting them in the slot of a chocolate machine that stood on the platform. He waited. A bar of pistachio nougat dropped through the flap at the bottom.

'It's cold,' he said, peeling the tinfoil from the half-frozen bar of nougat. 'Let's go inside.'

They opened the door to the waiting room and stepped inside. A fire smouldered and spat in the hearth and a tall, pale-painted long-case clock, with a deep and resonant tick, marked the passing seconds.

'What do you want?' said a voice. Greta turned. There stood the Stationmaster, a large man with a bristling beard and red face, cracked by the wind. 'Well?' he demanded.

'Where are we exactly?' said Greta, slowly backing away.

'If you don't know that, then you've no business being here,' said the Stationmaster, advancing on the twins.

'Aren't we near to something?' asked Feliks.

'You're not near anything,' said the Stationmaster. 'How did you get here?'

'On the train,' replied Greta.

'Where are your mother and father?' demanded the man.

'They ran away,' said Feliks.

'Don't get smart with me, boy,' said the Stationmaster.

'He's telling the truth,' said Greta. 'Our mother and father ran off and left us, and our aunt died.'

'Is there a village near here?' asked Feliks. 'Somewhere we can stay?'

'No village. No town. Nothing to see,' said the man. 'Only this station.'

'Then why build a station?' asked Feliks.

The Stationmaster growled. 'That's none of your business, is it?'

'What are you going to do to us?' asked Greta.

'Do to you?' said the Stationmaster. 'What do you think I'm going to do?'

'Murder us?' asked Feliks.

The Stationmaster eyed the boy suspiciously. 'Murder you? Of course I'm not going to murder you. I'm going to lock you in my office and when the first train comes through, I'm putting you both on it.'

'A train to where?' asked Feliks.

'Who cares?' said the Stationmaster. 'No business of mine, is it?' He marched the twins out of the waiting room and along the station platform.

'Run!' screamed Greta, squirming free from the man's grasp.

'Not so fast,' he grunted, seizing Feliks tightly with both hands. Feliks struggled, but the man held him fast. Greta had no choice. She kicked the Stationmaster sharply in the leg and he released his grip.

'Now, Feliks!' yelled Greta, grabbing Feliks by the hand.

'Come here!' shrieked the Stationmaster.

'Don't look back!' cried Greta, as the twins ran from the railway platform and into the woods beyond. It was a forest of tall pine trees and silver birch. As they ran, they passed a faded wooden sign, which had been nailed to a tree.

'Bears,' read Feliks breathlessly. 'Beware!'

'I expect it's to scare people off,' said Greta.

'But who wants to scare people off?' panted Feliks.

Greta smiled. 'If we don't carry on the way we're going

we'll never find out, will we?'

'Wait for me,' moaned Feliks, following his sister deeper into the forest.

A whistle blew, and Greta thought she could make out the sound of a distant bell, chiming through the trees. They stumbled onwards, scrambling over rocks, rough as sandpaper with green lichen.

'We can't let him catch us,' said Greta.

But the Stationmaster had long since given up the chase. He walked quickly along the platform and into his office, where he picked up the telephone and dialled.

'It's me,' he growled. 'Two of them. A boy and a girl. I thought you'd want to know. They're on their way.'

CHAPTER TWENTY-THREE

'**I**'m hungry,' moaned Feliks.

'You're always hungry,' said Greta.

The forest was dark and forbidding and smelt strongly of rotting leaves. Exactly the sort of place, thought Feliks, from which unwary children seldom re-emerge. His pace began slowing to a crawl.

'Can't we stop and eat?' he begged.

'All right,' said Greta. 'But we can't stop for long. I think we need to get as far away from the station as we can. And who knows, there might really be bears.'

They sat on a rock and Feliks took his bar of pistachio nougat from his pocket.

'There's not much left,' he said, passing the bar to Greta. She pulled the remaining nugget of nougat in half, and chewed silently, lost in thought. It seemed a lifetime since they had journeyed to the Sunken City. But it had only been two days.

Greta turned to her brother. 'It's funny how so many bad things can happen in such a short time.'

'Where are we, do you think?' asked Feliks.

'I don't know,' said Greta. 'But we should keep walking. It's getting cold.'

'What if we never come out the other side?' asked Feliks, imagining for a moment that they would live out their whole lives trapped inside the forest.

Greta frowned. 'Of course we'll come out the other side,' she said. 'Forests don't go on forever. There's always another side.'

They trudged on, the cold gnawing at their bones as a fine sprinkling of snow scattered down around them. As Greta had predicted, the trees soon began to thin out and a clearing became visible up ahead.

'There,' she said triumphantly. 'You see? I told you.'

It took a moment for their eyes to grow accustomed to the light after the gloom of the forest. They had arrived at the edge of a small village of half-beamed houses with thatched roofs.

Greta stepped from the trees onto a cobbled street.

'I don't like it,' said Feliks, but nevertheless followed his sister onto the cobbles.

It seemed that the houses had not been lived in for

many years. Leafless branches rattled like bones in the breeze as the twins walked through the heart of the abandoned village. The street seemed familiar somehow, like one they had perhaps visited in dreams, but a place that did not quite belong in the real world.

'It's like a village, but not a village,' said Greta, following a set of tramlines embedded in the cobbled street that led to a castellated archway.

'I know this place,' said Feliks. 'What I mean is, I *think* I know this place.'

'How can you?' replied Greta. 'We've never been here before.' She tapped at the wall of one of the buildings and a lump of plaster crumbled to the ground, revealing a patch of wood behind. 'It's not real,' said Greta, staggering backwards. 'It's not stone; it's just plaster and wood.'

'Somebody's watching us,' said Feliks quietly.

'You're imagining things,' said Greta.

'No,' said Feliks, pointing to a window. 'Somebody is watching us.'

As Greta looked up, a curtain twitched.

'It's just the wind,' she said, uncertainly, as they

carried on walking.

They reached a river which surged past the edge of the village, gushing over rocks before crashing down in a small waterfall beyond the archway.

Feliks was struggling to understand why the tramlines that ran along the cobbles came from nowhere and went nowhere.

'There really are people watching us,' whispered Greta, suddenly sensing shadows moving between the buildings.

'That's what I said,' whispered Feliks. 'You didn't believe me.'

'What do you want me to say?' replied Greta through gritted teeth. 'You were right all along. And now we're going to be murdered. Is that what you want me to say?'

A figure lurched out from the trees into the market square.

'The Stationmaster,' said Feliks, clutching hold of Greta's arm.

The twins backed away slowly. But their way was barred by a tall, heavily built man standing behind them.

'It's too late,' whispered Greta. 'This is the end.'

'Or it could be a beginning,' said a familiar voice.

The twins turned and there stood Morbide.

'It's me,' said Morbide with a grin. 'You're safe now.'

'M-Morbide,' stammered Greta. 'Then it was you who sent the timetable!'

Feliks could not speak. It felt as though his legs were buckling beneath him and he clung to Greta's arm to keep himself upright.

The figures that had lurked in the shadows stepped out onto the cobbles. There before the twins stood Doctor Kessler, Vladek and Gabor, the Blind Butcher and Bullfrog. And suddenly, with a fluttering of feathers, Karloff appeared and settled on Feliks's shoulder, nibbling at his ear.

'He flew back to Mrs Moritz,' explained Morbide.

'Olga let him escape,' said Feliks. Morbide nodded.

There was a loud rustle and panting from the trees, and a large woman appeared with a basket of food.

'You could have waited for me,' she bellowed.

'My wife,' said the Stationmaster apologetically.

'How did you all come here?' asked Greta. 'Where are we?'

The Stationmaster laughed. 'I looked out of my office

one night,' he said, 'and I saw a man standing on the platform. Horrible great thing he was, to look at. Leering in, he was. So I ran out the back and I said to my wife, "Am I going mad, or is that the Blind Butcher standing out there on the platform?"'

'That's right.' His wife nodded. 'He did. He did say that.'

'Then she starts screaming,' continued the Stationmaster. '"The Blind Butcher! The Blind Butcher, he's going to cut us all to ribbons with his great cleaver."'

'I did say that,' said the Stationmaster's wife, gurgling like a drain as she laughed. '"Cut us all to ribbons," I said.'

'It was Doctor Kessler's idea to come here,' said Bullfrog, unscrewing the lid of a silver hip flask and taking a sip. 'After Von Merhart was killed and Morbide was arrested, there wasn't a place for us monsters in Schwartzgarten.'

'Where's China Doll?' asked Greta suddenly.

'She's not dead, is she?' said Feliks.

'Gone funny in the brains,' said Bullfrog, tapping on the side of his head with the stubby tip of his index finger.

'Be quiet,' grunted Morbide.

'She keeps herself locked up in that tower,' said Doctor

Kessler, pointing to a turret built into the wall of the castellated archway. 'She gets melancholy. Even in the middle of the day it's dark here. The trees, you understand.'

China Doll appeared at the window of the tower, smiling sadly at the group below. Somehow, though it was barely possible for the twins to believe, she looked paler than before.

'The darkness,' said Bullfrog. 'It gets to you. As if the forest is strangling the life out of the village. Sometimes I lie in bed and dream that the roots of the trees burst up through the soil, and slither up along the street to my front door.'

Doctor Kessler sighed and shook his head. 'It's taken its toll on all of us. But China Doll, worst of all.'

'What he means,' said Bullfrog, 'is it's not the same as living in Schwartzgarten. But we had no choice. Things were too bad in the city, so we had to come here.'

'We have sentry duty,' said Morbide, as he led the children through the trees. 'Up there.' He pointed to a platform, which had been erected between two silver birch trees.

'We ring the bell in case of danger. You can see as far as the railway halt. Further, on a clear day.'

'Did you escape from prison again?' asked Greta.

'I did,' said Morbide. 'There's not a cell that can keep me away from my beautiful China Doll.'

There was no running water, not even a well, so water was carried in a bucket from the fast-flowing river. The village was without electricity, so candlelight was the only way of illuminating the houses. Even in the daytime it was so dark that they needed candles. Bullfrog had insisted that they needed a telephone in case of emergency, and this was housed in the morgue at the edge of the village, with a line trailing across the forest floor to connect with the station.

'People were making trouble for Von Merhart,' explained Morbide as he dipped the bucket in the river, filling it with icy water. 'He had this village built so he could make his movies away from prying eyes. But not a single frame of film was ever shot here.' He lumbered back inside his thatched house, followed by the twins. 'He was murdered before he ever had a chance.'

Morbide's tiny kitchen had meagre provisions, hardly

enough to keep him fed and healthy, let alone two visitors.

'We don't have much,' said Morbide. 'Other than the things we carry back from the station. Things that fall off the trains,' he added with a wink.

'And you really trust the Stationmaster?' asked Greta.

'He's a friend,' said Morbide. 'A good friend. Without his help, we would've starved here.'

Morbide lit the stove. He cut thick slices of peppered sausage and tossed them into the sizzling pan.

But Feliks was troubled as they sat down to supper and this rarely happened when he was about to eat. He knew that they could not remain in the village.

'We have to go back to Schwartzgarten,' he said at last. 'As long as Olga is free we'll never feel truly safe. We have to show the police our evidence.'

Greta nodded in agreement. 'And we need to find Ostrovsky. Maybe then we can prove that Olga has been planning to murder us.'

CHAPTER TWENTY-FOUR

T he twins sat patiently as Morbide applied putty to change their facial features. He used mortician's wax to extend Greta's nose and cotton balls to pad out Feliks's cheeks. They had both been given wigs and padded coats to disguise their normal shape; costumes which had been stored in the morgue.

'Can't we look more like monsters?' said Greta, peering into a shattered shard of mirror glass. She reached into her coat pocket and retrieved the fangs that Duttlinger had made for her.

Morbide smiled.

'You need to look as ordinary as possible,' he said. 'If you look like monsters you'll be rounded up and arrested at once.' He opened a box and took out a set of false teeth. 'Try these for size instead.'

Feliks placed the teeth inside his mouth, secured them in position and smiled at his reflection.

'There's a goods train that comes through Stoller tonight,' said the Stationmaster. 'That's the safest way to get the twins back to Schwartzgarten.'

That night Greta and Feliks climbed up into the mail wagon of the goods train, leaving Karloff in Morbide's care.

'In case your noses begin to come loose,' said Morbide, passing each twin a small bottle of liquid gum. He hugged the twins goodbye and pressed ten crowns into Greta's hand.

The Stationmaster slid the door of the wagon closed, allowing just enough of a gap to let the children see out.

'Take this,' he said, passing Feliks a bar of pistachio nougat. 'Rations. And a map of Schwartzgarten to help you find your way around the city without being spotted.'

Morbide waved as the train pulled slowly from the station. 'Be careful,' he called quietly. 'Don't trust anybody.'

Feliks settled down against the mailbags and closed his eyes. But Greta stayed awake, peering through the gap in the wagon door. Grey wolves ran through deserted forests, glimpsed between the trees, disturbed by the hiss and roar of the passing steam train.

At last even Greta felt her eyes closing, lulled into

sleep by the gentle rocking motion of the wagon.

It was early morning when Greta awoke at the sound of the train whistle shrieking. She peered outside. The train was slowing down as the trees thinned out and the city of Schwartzgarten came into view; the air was heavy with the smell of malt from the distant brewery.

'Wake up,' said Greta, shaking Feliks gently. 'We're almost there.'

Feliks sat up and knelt beside Greta, staring out through the crack in the door as the train drew slowly to a halt.

'This is our chance,' said Greta, picking up the box of evidence. 'We need to get off now before anyone finds us here.'

Together they pulled back the door of the wagon. They jumped from the train, and carefully made their way across the tracks, picking their way between stationary carriages and engines until they found themselves on the threshold of Schwartzgarten's Industrial District. Feliks took out the bar of nougat.

'We'll need that to sustain us,' said Greta, snatching the nougat from Feliks and hiding it away safely in her pocket.

Greta unfolded the map, hidden from sight behind

a railway carriage. 'We need to make sure that nobody spots us,' she said, drawing out the safest route across the city, with the pencil from Feliks's pocketbook.

It was a cold, clear day. There were swirls of crackled ice on the windows of motor cars and an aroma of freshly roasted coffee and gingerbread in the air as they made their way into the heart of Schwartzgarten.

'Police,' whispered Greta, as a constable crossed the tramlines in front of them. 'We have to be careful, they might be hunting for us.'

'In here,' said Feliks, tugging his sister by the arm, and leading her into the pastry shop on the corner of Edvardplatz.

<hr>

'It's crème pâtissière,' said Feliks.

Greta stared at her brother blankly. 'What is?'

'This. What we're eating,' said Feliks, pointing at the pastry on the table in front of him. 'They make it from eggs, milk, cream and sugar.'

'Fascinating,' said Greta. She stared out of the window, onto Edvardplatz. 'Where do you think Olga is now?'

'I don't know,' said Feliks. 'But wherever she is, she's probably still plotting to murder us.' He bit into another pastry and considered matters, his fears temporarily soothed by the friendly hiss and guttural gurgle of the coffee machine.

'We've got to be brave,' said Greta. 'It's what Aunt Gisela would say.'

'It's difficult trying to be brave when someone wants to kill you,' said Feliks mournfully.

The windows of the pastry shop rattled as a tram thundered past outside.

'What are we going to do?' asked Feliks. 'How are we going to find Ostrovsky?'

'I don't know,' said Greta. 'But I'm certain that Aunt Gisela would have known.'

———◆———

The snow in the Schwartzgarten Municipal Cemetery was still thick under foot as Feliks and Greta trod the path towards Aunt Gisela's grave. They stood and stared in silence at the solitary tombstone. The flowers had been eaten by rats.

'I wish she was still here,' whispered Feliks. Greta nodded. She snapped the head from a winter rose and laid it gently on the grass at the foot of the grave.

The twins picked their way carefully from the cemetery and across the Princess Euphenia Bridge and into the New Town. As they reached the northern bank of the river, jostling through the crowds in front of the Emperor Xavier Hotel, Greta reached up to adjust her wig and in doing so, knocked off her false nose of mortician's wax. It was unfortunate that this was witnessed by a small girl in the surging crowd, who stared at Greta in open-mouthed surprise. Greta looked down at the girl's jacket and in horror she noticed the glittering pin of the Van Veenen Adventure Society.

'You're Greta Mortenberg,' gasped the girl. 'The one that Olga Van Veenen is searching for.'

Greta shook her head and pushed the wax nose back into place.

'Nobody's looking for me,' she said.

But the girl turned to point at a handbill, which had been pasted onto a nearby telegraph pole.

'It's you,' said the girl.

Above a photograph of the twins and printed in red were the words: RUNAWAYS. MAY BE UNSOUND OF MIND. DO NOT APPROACH BUT TELEPHONE MISS O. VAN VEENEN ON SCHWARTZGARTEN 532 AT YOUR EARLIEST CONVENIENCE.

Before Greta could do anything to stop the girl, she turned and ran towards the nearest telephone kiosk.

'We have to go now!' cried Greta, seizing Feliks by the arm. 'There are spies everywhere.'

They hurried to the banks of the River Schwartz, only to find themselves in the middle of another crowd. The police were dragging something heavy from the river. The crowds parted and two constables laid a body on the ground.

'It's Otto Ostrovsky!' cried Greta, turning to her brother.

'No, no,' said a man with a bald head who stood beside them.

'That is Claudius Estridge, Olga's publisher,' gasped Feliks.

The words had barely escaped his lips when the twins

saw a familiar figure pushing his way through the crowds towards them.

'It's Valentin,' gasped Feliks as the man pressed the trigger in the handle of his pinstripe umbrella and the poisoned spike appeared in the tip.

'We've got to get away!' screamed Greta.

'Where can we go?' shouted Feliks.

'To the Department of Police,' said Greta. 'Ostrovsky's dead, but we've still got our evidence.' By the time Valentin had freed himself from the crowd the twins were halfway towards the Princess Euphenia Bridge. Suddenly the Superintendent's motor van loomed into view, dribbling oil as it lurched across the cobbles.

'They're all looking for us,' gasped Greta. 'We're not safe anywhere.'

Feliks turned to see Valentin climbing onto a motorbike.

'That's my bike!' protested a delivery boy, hurrying from the Emperor Xavier Hotel.

'Not any more,' said Valentin, giving the boy a savage shove. He revved the engine, which gave a guttural death rattle. The exhaust belched out a choking cloud of black smoke.

'Run!' screamed Greta.

The Superintendent's van careered erratically along the cobbled street and onto the bridge. She craned her head out of the window.

'Slow down, my little poppets,' she bawled at the top of her voice. 'Olga Van Veenen's out of her mind with worry. Count yourself lucky you've got a guardian who cares for you like she does.'

But the twins did not slacken their pace. The Department of Police was just visible in the distance, on the opposite bank of the river.

'Quickly, Feliks,' cried Greta.

The Superintendent was beckoning to Valentin as she bumped along in her motor van. At last all became clear to the twins, as though the final piece of the puzzle had slipped into place.

'That's where Olga got all the children from,' cried Greta.

'Yes,' shouted back Feliks. 'From the Reformatory.'

Valentin roared across the bridge on the motorbike, clutching his umbrella tightly under his arm like a jousting knight of old. Feliks was struggling to keep up with Greta, and Valentin chose his moment to lunge at the boy with the umbrella. But what Feliks lacked in speed he more than made up for in agility. He jumped and the poisoned tip of the umbrella grazed across the pavement, sending sparks high into the air. As Feliks stumbled on, the box of evidence slipped from his hands and its contents tipped out into the gutter. The motorbike swung round three hundred and sixty degrees as Valentin prepared for a second strike.

Greta turned back for the fallen pieces of evidence.

'It's too late,' cried Feliks. 'Leave it. They'll have to believe us now.'

Valentin swerved past on the motorbike, snatching at Feliks's coat, ripping the sleeve. But Feliks wrenched himself from Valentin's grasp and ran inside the open door of the Department of Police, closely followed by Greta, who slammed the door behind her and ran with Feliks to the desk.

'What do you think you're—' began the desk sergeant, glaring at the twins.

'He's going to kill us!' shrieked Greta.

'Who is?' asked the desk sergeant. 'What are you talking about?'

'A man. Outside,' panted Greta. 'He's trying to murder us with his umbrella.'

Wearily, the desk sergeant picked up the telephone and dialled.

'There are two children here, Inspector,' said the man. 'They claim that someone is trying to murder them. With an umbrella, if you can believe such a thing.'

The door swung open and the Inspector of Police appeared as Valentin came crashing inside.

'What's all this?' barked the Inspector. 'What's going on?'

Valentin gasped, fighting to regain his breath.

'That's the man,' said Feliks, pointing wildly at Valentin, hardly able to speak.

'He's the one,' insisted Greta. 'He's the one that's trying to murder us.'

'A murderer, eh?' said the Inspector. He stared hard at the twins. 'Don't I know you?'

Just then, the door opened again and Olga Van Veenen swept into the room, a silver fox fur wrapped tightly around her shoulders. Her eyes alighted on the twins.

'Oh, my darling angels!' she trilled. 'I thought you

were lost to me. Lost in the big, dark city.' She turned to the Inspector. 'Do forgive them if they caused you any trouble. I'm quite convinced the cold weather has unsettled their adorable little brains.'

'Quite possible,' said the Inspector. 'I've seen it take less to turn a child quite peculiar.'

'Don't listen to her,' moaned Greta. 'She's the one who wants us dead.'

The Inspector of Police leant down to face her. He smiled and twirled his moustache between his fingertips. 'When I was a boy I used to read the Detective Durning stories,' he began slowly. 'I used to lie in bed under the quilt with a pocket torch and read when I should have been sleeping. And sometimes I got muddled in my mind; muddled about what was true and what was only make-believe.'

'But we're not imagining anything,' said Greta. 'She wants us dead because we know her deep, dark secret.' Olga smiled.

'And what deep dark secret is that?' asked the Inspector patiently.

Greta stared at the man. He smiled back at her. He didn't believe a word she said, which was frustrating, as every word she uttered was true. In spite of this, Greta still related all the details of their perilous adventure, taking great care to describe the ingenious labyrinth that had been constructed beneath Castle Van Veenen.

'This needs further investigation, I think,' said Olga with a frown and a flutter of her eyelashes. 'These are very serious allegations.'

'Very well,' agreed the Inspector with an apologetic nod. 'If only to prove these children wrong.'

'Of course, Inspector,' said Olga. 'My private railway carriage is entirely at your disposal. We must travel together to Castle Van Veenen.'

CHAPTER TWENTY-FIVE

'**We've got** to be prepared,' whispered Greta to Feliks as they set off from Schwartzgarten's Imperial Railway Station. 'Olga will seize her first opportunity to try to murder us, so we need to be ready.'

They were fearful that they would not survive the journey back to Castle Van Veenen. But the twins were fortunate that an opportunity for Olga to slay them did not immediately present itself.

It was two days before the party reached the village of Burg, and all the time the twins remained under the watchful eye of the Inspector, three constables and Massimo, the Dobermann police dog.

Castle Van Veenen was every bit as grim as the twins remembered it. The Inspector of Police rapped hard on the iron knocker and the great door creaked open on its hinges. Greta took a deep breath. Her moment was rapidly approaching, her chance to prove that Olga Van Veenen had indeed plotted to kill them. As the twins stared into the gloom of the entrance hall, the face of an unfamiliar woman glowered back at them.

'What's going on?' demanded Greta. 'Where's Helga?

'Helga who?' the woman rasped. And then she caught sight of Olga Van Veenen and made a small and clumsy curtsy.

'I'm sorry, Miss Van Veenen,' said the woman. 'I didn't see you there. I didn't realise we were expecting you.'

'You weren't,' replied Olga. 'And yet, here we are.'

'But this isn't the housekeeper,' protested Greta.

Olga suppressed the smile that briefly played across her lips. 'Will you tell this poor unfortunate girl who you are?' she asked.

'Housekeeper,' said the woman.

'And have you ever seen these children before?' inquired the Inspector.

'Of course,' said the woman. 'They came to stay with Miss Van Veenen.'

'It's not true,' moaned Greta. 'We've never seen her before in our lives.'

The woman frowned down at the girl. 'That's a

wicked, evil thing to say,' she said. 'After all the happy times we spent together.'

'What a regrettable state of affairs,' said Olga quietly.

'She's lying!' screamed Greta. The blood-curdling exclamation reverberated so terrifyingly around the vast entrance hall of Castle Van Veenen that Olga held her hands to her ears.

'The girl's getting hysterical,' said the Inspector, taking Constable Schneider to one side. 'Get ready, just in case.'

'Yes, sir,' said the man, unscrewing the lid from a bottle of chloroform.

The Inspector turned back to the housekeeper. 'And how long have you been in employment here?' he asked.

'Twenty years,' said the woman.

The Inspector made a note in his pocketbook.

'So, you don't know anything about a mute housekeeper and her husband?' he said.

The woman shook her head and laughed.

'Just as I expected,' said the Inspector.

Suddenly, Feliks pushed past the housekeeper and ran into the hall.

'Slow down!' barked the Inspector. But Feliks did not slow down, and the Inspector had no choice but to follow him.

'Quickly,' said Feliks, as he led the Inspector, panting and gasping, to the library beyond the Hall of Ancestors. He ran across the creaking wooden floor towards the panelled wall. 'Here,' he said, 'this is the secret door where we escaped from the cavern.'

The Inspector turned to Olga, but she simply tapped her finger gently against the side of her head.

'Quite deluded of course,' she whispered.

Feliks pressed hard against the panel, expecting it to spring open easily. It did not. 'Maybe it was this panel instead,' he said, pressing a neighbouring panel in the wall. As before, nothing happened. But Feliks was not to be defeated so easily. 'That was the way we came out,' he said, 'but maybe there isn't a way in.'

'Now we come to the truth of the matter,' sighed the Inspector.

'No,' said Feliks with a smile, 'what I mean is, we have to go down the same way as we did before. Through the bookcase.' He ran to the great bookcase on the opposite wall, and cast his eyes along the rows of leather-bound books. At last, his gaze settled on one particular volume: *Recipes from the North-Eastern Region of the Country.*

'You see?' He tugged at the spine of the book, which moved easily. But there was no grinding of cogs and the bookcase did not slide back into the wall. Instead, Feliks was able to pull the book clear from the shelf.

'It's just a book,' said Greta, puzzled, taking it from him and examining it closely.

The Inspector rolled his eyes and tutted. 'Just a book,' he repeated.

'There is a secret passage,' protested Feliks, his collar damp with perspiration and clinging uncomfortably to his throat. But even he was beginning to doubt that there really was a secret entrance to the chambers below. He half-feared that he had dreamt the whole thing.

'I don't understand,' said Greta, 'it doesn't make sense.'

'There's only one way to settle this,' said Olga. 'We must tear the bookcase from the wall.'

'But the damage it will cause—' protested the Inspector.

Olga raised her hand. 'Not another word, dear Inspector,' she said.

The Inspector reddened around the cheeks and he mopped his forehead with his coat sleeve.

'I can see you're a very curious man,' Olga continued. 'The very best detectives are celebrated for their curiosity.'

'It would be rude for me to say that isn't so,' said the Inspector, nodding in agreement.

'You won't be happy until you've searched to make certain that there is no secret doorway leading to a subterranean cavern,' said Olga, motioning with her gloved hand towards the bookcase.

'If you're quite sure?' said the Inspector.

'Quite sure,' insisted Olga. 'Valentin, fetch a hammer.'

Valentin, who had been lurking in a corner of the room, leafing through a crumbling volume devoted to medieval instruments of torture, strode from the library. He returned with a large claw hammer, which the three constables used to prise back the bookcase. To Feliks's astonishment there was nothing behind but a solid stone wall.

'It was necessary,' said Olga sadly. 'To prove to you,

dear Inspector, how disturbed these precious angels truly are.'

'Don't believe her,' said Greta desperately. 'She's lying to you.'

'What do you want me to do?' asked the Inspector of Police. 'Arrest Miss Van Veenen and sling her in a cell?'

'Yes, please,' said Feliks.

'Obviously, I was being sarcastic,' said the Inspector, twisting his moustache between finger and thumb for dramatic effect.

'They're overtired,' said Olga quietly. 'I shall take care of the unfortunate little darlings. Peace and quiet is all they need to restore the balance of their troubled minds.'

'It's a lie,' cried Greta. 'She's lying!'

'Quiet now,' said the Inspector. 'No need to be getting hysterical again.'

'But she is trying to kill us, honestly,' said Feliks.

The Inspector laughed sourly. 'Whenever a little boy says "honestly" then I know he's telling me lies,' he said. 'Now let that be an end to all this nonsense.' He turned and smiled at Olga. 'And perhaps...I hardly like to ask—'

Olga smiled serenely. 'Anything, dear Inspector,' she

said, taking the man's hand and patting it affectionately.

The Inspector of Police coughed nervously and the tips of his moustache began to quiver.

'If you could sign a book for my nephew?'

'And your nephew's name?' asked Olga.

'Boris,' said the Inspector and coughed again. 'Same as mine.'

Olga raised her eyebrows and smiled at the Inspector. She reached up and took a copy of *The Skull That Grinned* from an undamaged bookshelf, which she opened and signed with a flourish. 'Darling Inspector,' she gushed, pressing the book into the Inspector's trembling hands.

The Inspector turned to face the twins. 'I ought to charge you for wasting police time,' he growled.

Greta's heart beat heavily in her chest. She struggled to speak. 'But what about the other missing children?' she insisted.

'And what do you know about missing children?' asked the Inspector.

'You're confusing fact and fiction, poor darling Greta,' said Olga with a crocodile grin.

The Inspector turned to Olga. 'You did a kind thing,

taking these children out of the Reformatory,' he said. 'You gave them new clothes, a roof over their heads. And how do they thank you? Like this, that's how.'

'Yes,' replied Olga. 'It has been a very upsetting time.'

'Sometimes this happens,' continued the Inspector. 'Sometimes a well-meaning and well-respected person such as yourself comes along, fishes round in the Reformatory for Maladjusted Children and plucks out two children just like these. I'm not blaming nobody, but sometimes what happens is they end up getting even more maladjusted than they were to begin with.'

'I'm sure if I were to try again—' began Olga.

The Inspector rubbed his hands together and chuckled. 'That's the point I'm making. The very point. They'll just keep getting more and more maladjusted, day after maladjusted day, until sooner or later they'll be so unhinged they'll probably murder you in your bed. You just see if they don't.'

The confidence began to drain from Olga's face. 'What exactly are you saying, Inspector?' she asked uncertainly.

'What I'm saying is this,' said the Inspector. 'I'm

going to take these little roaches and sling them behind bars, where they should have been locked up all along.'

'Yes, please,' said Greta, clutching hold of the Inspector's arm. Incarceration in the Reformatory was preferable to being left alone with Olga.

Feliks nodded enthusiastically.

The Inspector sighed. 'You see? What did I tell you? As maladjusted as you'd ever hope to find.' He seized the twins by the lapels of their jackets.

But Olga placed her hand on the Inspector's arm and smiled. 'That really won't be necessary. I have to travel back to Schwartzgarten for a meeting with my agent. I am quite certain that returning to the city will help to settle their troubled minds, as long as they have me to look after them.'

The Inspector gazed into her eyes: she fluttered her eyelashes and his heart fluttered back.

'Very well, then,' said the Inspector. 'If you're certain?'

'I am,' said Olga sweetly.

The Inspector stared down at the twins. 'You don't know how fortunate you are. To have someone that loves you to death like your kind, sweet guardian.'

Olga kissed Greta on the forehead, and gently squeezed Feliks's hand.

'It's enough to make a man's heart bleed with joy,' said the Inspector, taking the bottle of chloroform from Constable Schneider and replacing the lid. 'To see the goodness in this world. I'll escort you back to Schwartzgarten, of course. To make sure your little angels don't take wing again.'

And so, trembling with the cold, their minds paralysed by fear, the twins were delivered back into the care of Olga Van Veenen.

CHAPTER TWENTY-SIX

The twins stared in despair from the window of Olga's private railway carriage, which was conveying the party on the return journey to Schwartzgarten.

It was dinner time, but the twins had no appetite. The Inspector of Police cut into a thick rump steak as Olga took a sip of champagne. She laughed as bubbles tickled her mouth, and the Inspector watched, utterly bewitched. He peered adoringly into Olga's eyes, and imagined how wonderful his life would be if he were married to such a woman and not the wife who loathed and taunted him, and to whom he was shortly to return.

'Life's a cruel beast,' he said with passion.

'I quite agree, dear Inspector,' said Olga, directing an acid smile towards the twins that hinted strongly at the cruelty yet to come.

Constable Schneider stepped into the carriage, clearly in some agitation. He was phantom white and the sleeve of his uniform had been badly ripped at the cuff.

'What is it?' barked the Inspector, taking a sip of

champagne. 'Can't you see we're occupied?

'Massimo's loose,' hissed the Constable. 'He got out of his cage.'

'Well, get him back in again,' said the Inspector, smiling at Olga in the vague hope that he had impressed her with his command of the situation.

Olga gave a faint smile of encouragement, and took another sip of champagne.

'You're the only one that can calm him,' insisted Constable Schneider.

The Inspector grunted. 'What hope is there of you locking up raving murderous madmen,' he said, 'if you can't keep one damn mutt under lock and key?' He made his apologies and picked up the remnants of his steak, which he wrapped in a napkin, to coax Massimo back into his cage. The Constable followed him out, leaving the twins alone with Olga and Valentin.

'Why don't you just kill us now and get it over with?' asked Feliks.

'Because people would ask awkward questions,' replied Olga. 'But then, as I often say, accidents do happen,' she added with an optimistic smile.

She waved a hand to Valentin, who stood silently at the far end of the carriage.

'Take my two darling children to their berth,' said Olga. 'And make sure they're locked up safely out of harm's way.'

Olga did not even watch as the twins were ushered from the carriage, instead taking another sip of champagne and lighting one of her purple-tipped cigarettes. Valentin pushed the twins along the corridor towards their berth. Up ahead could be heard the unmistakable bark and growl of Massimo, as he snapped first at the steak and then at the Constable, savouring the taste of each with obvious pleasure. The carriage shook as it rattled over a drift of snow and as the twins passed Olga's private bathroom, the door swung open. The window had been pulled up to ventilate the room and an icy blast whipped along the carriage. Valentin growled and pushed the door shut.

Suddenly, Massimo's bark grew louder, and the hound lurched into view, dragging Constable Schneider behind him.

'Stop him at once!' ordered the Inspector.

But it was no use. Massimo bounded along the

corridor, giving Greta a slobbery lick in passing and hurled himself at Valentin, pushing the man backwards into Olga's dining saloon, followed by the Inspector and the Constable.

'This is our chance!' hissed Greta. She opened the door to Olga's bathroom and dragged Feliks in behind her.

'Lock the door,' she whispered, struggling to open the window wide.

'What are we going to do?' asked Feliks as he turned the key in the door.

Greta climbed up onto the bathtub, steadying herself against the window frame.

'We're going to escape, that's what we're going to do,' she replied, leaning her head out of the window and pulling herself up so she sat on the narrow sill.

'Look out for tunnels,' warned Feliks.

Greta leant from the window, reaching for a handhold on the outside of the carriage. She climbed up to stand on the sill and disappeared from view.

Reluctantly, Feliks followed his sister's example.

'We'll be killed,' he shouted, struggling to be heard

above the roar of the speeding steam engine.

'And we'll be killed if we stay where we are,' Greta shouted back, making her way up the iron rungs leading to the roof of the carriage. 'Now climb!'

Feliks followed Greta's orders obediently and together they slowly made their way up onto the roof.

'Lie down and crawl,' yelled Greta. 'Press yourself against the roof so you don't get blown down!'

The train whistle sounded, and a choking cloud of steam enveloped the twins.

'Look!' screamed Feliks, as the Inspector of Police's head emerged through the steam at the far end of the carriage roof.

'Thought you could give us the slip, did you?' cried the Inspector. 'Stop where you are and no harm will come to you.'

But the twins had no intention of stopping. They knew that if they did, harm would certainly come to them.

'I think I'm going to be sick,' moaned Feliks, desperately clinging to the train roof though his fingers were fast turning white in the bitter cold.

'If you'd read Olga's books you'd know how to deal

with adventures when they come along,' said Greta.

'We've got to get off,' yelled Feliks.

'I know that!' cried Greta, accidentally inhaling a large, passing fly. They were engulfed by a cloud of black smoke as the train passed through a tunnel. Greta tugged at Feliks's arm, and together they climbed down the iron ladder at the front of the carriage, cloaked by the choking steam.

'Where are they?' screamed the Inspector as the train emerged from the tunnel. His moustache twitched under the weight of tunnel soot.

The twins had vanished.

'Maybe they fell off,' suggested Constable Schneider, climbing up beside the Inspector and looking back down the line, searching for any sign of the twins.

Meanwhile, Greta and Feliks were still gripping tightly to the ladder. Greta was just able to peer in through the window of Olga's private saloon. The Inspector of Police and the Constable had made their way from the roof of the carriage and had returned inside.

'Fetch Massimo!' shouted the Inspector.

'We've only just locked him up again,' said the

Constable, his voice warbling with fear.

'I said fetch him!' bawled the Inspector.

'What is it? What has happened?' demanded Olga. 'What has become of my darling angels?'

'They escaped,' replied the Inspector. 'Slippery as eels those two.'

'Fools!' shrieked Olga. 'Find them at once!'

The Inpsector sighed and the love died in his heart. He put aside all dreams of an 'unfortunate accident' befalling his wife to make way for a possible wife number two.

Constable Schneider hurried off to the luggage van and returned with Massimo.

'Follow the scent, boy,' commanded the Inspector. 'Wherever they've got to, we'll sniff them out.'

'What are we going to do?' whispered Feliks, clinging to the outside of the carriage with his sister.

The sky had turned as dark as charcoal and the air had begun to freeze. The twins were fast losing feeling in their fingers as they clung to the metal rungs.

'We'll have to jump off,' said Feliks, suddenly taking control of the situation.

'But we don't know where we are,' said Greta. 'We

might be hundreds of miles from the nearest village. And anyway, we'd probably freeze to death or be killed by wolves before we ever got there.' Feliks smiled and the smile twitched into a laugh. Greta was certain that her brother was delirious from the cold.

'Look,' he said, nodding to the track up ahead but not daring to take a hand from the metal rungs to point. 'It's the station!'

Greta strained her eyes in the gloom. There before them was the station building of Stoller and the forest beyond.

The train gave a violent screech and bright orange sparks flew up from the tracks.

'It's stopping,' said Feliks. 'We have to get off before they reach the station.'

'I don't know that I can get off,' said Greta in alarm. 'I think my fingers have frozen.'

The steep ridge of a snowdrift swept high beside the train tracks. Without uttering another word Feliks gripped Greta's arm firmly. He wrenched her from the side of the train and together they jumped, sinking deep into the soft, undisturbed fall of snow.

They heard the squeal of brakes, as the train drew up alongside the deserted station platform. There were distant voices, and the whining bark of Massimo answered by wolf calls from deep inside the forest.

But the twins did not stop to listen. They made their way further into the trees, blindly trudging through the snow on their way back to the village and Morbide. Greta staggered against a soft, warm object and fought to regain her breath. The object snorted and exhaled, its breath enveloping the twins in unpleasant warmth.

'It's a bear,' hissed Greta, as the creature shook itself. 'Just run!' she screamed, crashing wildly through the undergrowth, reaching out for the low branches of a twisted elder tree.

'Not the trees,' yelled Feliks. 'Bears can climb trees better than we can.' He clutched at branches to steady himself as he ran to catch up with his sister, every icy breath tearing at his lungs.

Greta did not slacken her pace. 'We've got to get back to the village,' she said, as the bear lumbered towards her, slashing through the darkness with its razor claws.

There was a roar from above and a sudden flash of

light. The bear stood transfixed on the spot, staring up into the trees. A figure loomed high above the creature; a large figure, standing on tiptoe and arching its fingers. The bear whined as if mortally wounded, and lolloped away into the night.

'Morbide!' cried Greta, staring up at the sentry post. 'It's us, Morbide! Greta and Feliks.'

'Home and safe!' screamed Karloff, flying up through the branches.

CHAPTER TWENTY-SEVEN

China Doll, Bullfrog and the Stationmaster had arrived for dinner with Morbide and the twins, and sat drinking Doctor Kessler's plum brandy.

'We're not safe here,' said Morbide.

'But Von Merhart's map was destroyed when the studios burned down,' said China Doll who had recovered enough from her dark melancholia to eat a bowl of soup and half a buttered roll.

'That's right,' nodded Bullfrog. No one knows the village even exists.'

'And as long as no one knows we're here, we'll be safe,' said Feliks.

'And we've got the telephone for emergencies,' said Bullfrog. 'The Stationmaster will warn us if there are enemies on the prowl.'

But Greta was not so certain. 'It's only a matter of time before someone finds us,' she whispered. 'We need to keep moving on.'

'You'll be safe enough when the snows come,' said the

Stationmaster. 'You think the snow is bad now, but you haven't lived. One day it's grey and dirty and the snow's up as far as your shins, then the next day, just like that,' he clicked his fingers, 'it's so deep you can't breathe in without sucking snowflakes up your nostrils.' He rubbed his hands at the thought of it. 'Stoke up the fire and keep out the cold, I say.'

The heavy snow did not come for another week, but when it did it arrived as unexpectedly as the Stationmaster had predicted. The twins and Morbide staggered through the deep fall, which muffled all sound. A row of black ravens huddled for warmth on an ice-bound branch above the frozen river. A wolf howled from the forest.

'The wolves are getting hungry,' said Bullfrog, appearing from the house. 'Bad sign. You know where they're going to come next, don't you, looking for meat?'

'Be quiet,' growled Morbide, as he attempted to break the thick river ice.

As Feliks prepared food in Morbide's house, Greta trudged off through the trees. No matter how far away from Schwartzgarten they seemed, she knew that she would never feel safe until Olga was locked behind bars.

Greta wandered all afternoon even as the light began to fail. By nightfall she had reached the edge of the forest, and found herself beside the dull grey walls of an ancient castle. It was pitch-black and as she stumbled out onto a dirt track she was blinded by the fierce glare of a motor car's headlights. The vehicle swerved, narrowly missing her, and came to a halt. It was an Estler-Spitz. At the wheel was none other than Count Sebastian Van Veenen, Olga's brother. Greta turned to run.

'Not so fast!' demanded Count Sebastian, climbing from the car. 'Ludovic, beckon the girl inside.'

A butler stepped from the castle and beckoned Greta forward with a gloved hand.

'Now keep up, child,' said Count Sebastian, mounting the castle steps. 'You are Greta Mortenberg, are you not?'

Greta nodded silently.

'Then what are you waiting for?'

Though she did not understand why, Greta felt compelled to follow the man, and this she did; up the steps and across the marble floor of the entrance hall.

'Are you going to murder me?' she asked.

'Oh yes, I shouldn't wonder,' said Count Sebastian, removing his scarf and leather motoring gauntlets. 'And where is your brother?'

'I'm not going to tell you,' said Greta with a scowl.

'I suppose if I'm going to murder you, I should probably get on with it,' said Count Sebastian, handing the gauntlets and scarf to Ludovic.

Greta moaned and backed away.

'Of course I'm not *really* going to murder you,' said Count Sebastian with a twinkling smile. 'Now keep up. I have something to show you.' He led Greta from the hall and through a grand carved doorway, into an enormous room with a polished wooden floor and a ceiling of gilded plasterwork. 'My ballroom!' he announced, gesturing to the vast room.

In the middle of the ballroom, beneath an enormous cut-glass chandelier, was a large wooden crate. At least, from a distance it appeared to be a crate, but as Greta and Count Sebastian approached, it became apparent that it was not a crate at all. It was a very solidly constructed box, a little taller than Count Sebastian himself. He opened a door in the side of the box and gestured politely for Greta to step inside.

'Are you going to chloroform me and have me shipped off to murderous bandits thousands and thousands of miles away?' asked Greta.

'Well, it's a thought I supp—' he began. But sensing that this was not the moment for flippancy, he stopped mid-sentence. 'I thought this might be of interest to you. Ludovic, please switch on the lights.' At the far end of the ballroom, Ludovic pressed an electric switch and suddenly the box glowed from within. 'Now please,' continued Count Sebastian, 'step inside and tell me what you think.'

Greta paused. Was Count Sebastian Van Veenen every bit as evil as his sister? And if he intended to kill her, why would he lure her into a wooden box? Surely there were easier ways to kill someone? Curiosity got the better of her and Greta passed through the doorway and into the box.

She found herself standing in Aunt Gisela's kitchen. Everything was exactly as she remembered. There was the kitchen table, the gas stove. There was even a box of

De Keyser cigars on the shelf of recipe books. She stared around in dumb-struck silence.

'Vanilla pudding?' said Count Sebastian, following Greta inside and lifting a bowl from the table. 'Try it. Your Aunt Gisela's very own recipe.'

Everything looked as it had always done in Aunt Gisela's day, but nothing felt the same. There was no aroma of oil of petunia, no sounds from the street outside. There was no Aunt Gisela. It was just as if Greta had wandered onto a set at the Von Merhart Movie Studios.

'It doesn't smell right,' she cried. 'Nothing's right at all.' She ran from the kitchen, slamming the door shut behind her.

'You don't like it?' asked Count Sebastian, following Greta out into the ballroom. 'I didn't mean to upset you. Your aunt's kitchen is exactly right in every respect. I employed the finest craftsmen in all of Schwartzgarten to reconstruct it for me. Everything is as she left it. I was an enormous admirer of your aunt's films. I bought all her worldly possessions when they were auctioned off after her death.' Count Sebastian bit his lip. He had no idea what to do next. 'I don't know many children,' he said at last, leading Greta into a smaller room, where Ludovic was setting a low table for tea beside a vast green sofa. Count Sebastian sat and motioned to Greta to sit beside him. 'I'm afraid I don't quite know what children like and what they don't like. My own failing of course. I don't suppose you're hungry?'

Greta nodded, though her stomach lurched uneasily.

'Excellent,' said Count Sebastian. 'I might not know much about children, but I do know all there is to know when it comes to the subject of coffee and cakes.'

'May I have peppermint cordial?' asked Greta.

'Certainly, certainly. And I shall join you in a glass,' said Count Sebastian, as Ludovic obediently hurried from the room. 'I'm fond of a glass of cordial myself. Revives the jaded palate and resuscitates the brain.'

Ludovic returned with two glasses of peppermint cordial and placed a silver cake stand on the table, piled high with cream cakes and macaroons. 'Excellent,' exhaled Count Sebastian, admiring the display of cakes. 'Please fetch me the family album, Ludovic.'

'Doesn't he mind running around all the time?' asked Greta.

'Not a bit of it,' replied Count Sebastian. 'Nothing he likes more. Doesn't even break a sweat.'

Ludovic hurried back swiftly, carrying a beautiful green leather photograph album, embossed with the cipher of the Van Veenen family.

'I have a story to relate to you,' began Count Sebastian. 'Any questions before we begin?'

'Is it true you're a murderer?' asked Greta, unable to hold the thought in her head any longer.

'May I inquire who it was that polluted your mind with such a scurrilous misapprehension?' said Count Sebastian.

'Does that mean you are a murderer or not?' said Greta, staring uncertainly into the eyes of her captor.

'Not,' said Count Sebastian, plucking a macaroon from the dish with a pair of silver tongs and dropping it onto his plate. 'I am not a murderer.'

'You didn't even kill someone by mistake?' continued Greta.

'Not as far as I can remember,' said Count Sebastian. 'And I'm sure I would remember.'

'Oh,' said Greta, feeling safe enough to sit more

comfortably on the sofa. 'She lied about that as well.'

'She?' repeated Count Sebastian, sipping from his glass of cordial. 'She who?'

'Olga,' said Greta.

'Of course,' laughed Count Sebastian. 'My delightful sister.' Greta flinched. 'A little joke. Not delightful at all. Monstrous.' Greta relaxed again. 'So, she's been telling tales, has she?'

'And then she tried to murder us,' added Greta.

'I rather feared that things would not end happily,' said Count Sebastian, turning the pages of the photograph album. 'I didn't grow up in a happy home,' he said sadly. 'Of course, as children we were indulged in every way. We had any gift and extravagance that money could buy. Not because our parents cared for us, you understand. They grasped every opportunity to prove that theirs was the richest family in all Schwartzgarten. My father once bought me a crocodile. What sort of father buys his son a crocodile?'

'Was it the crocodile that ate him?' asked Greta.

'It was,' replied Count Sebastian. 'And who could blame it? I certainly didn't.' He took a bite of a pistachio-caramel macaroon. 'And then one day shortly after, Olga tried to drown me in the bath.'

'How terrible,' said Greta.

Count Sebastian laughed. 'Not really,' he continued. 'I'd been expecting it, so I'd learnt to hold my breath underwater.'

'Maybe it was an accident?' said Greta, not believing it for a moment. 'Accidents do happen sometimes.'

'My dear girl.' Count Sebastian shook his head and took another bite of the macaroon. 'You don't accidentally hold someone underwater for two minutes. After the first minute it's no longer an accident but murderous intent. Do try the macaroons.'

'I'm allergic to almonds,' explained Greta.

'Then have a cream cake instead,' said Count Sebastian.

Greta helped herself to a caramel cream pastry.

As Count Sebastian turned a page in the album, Greta's attention was arrested by a startling photograph. A child stared back at her, a small, strange boy with bug-like eyes. Count Sebastian laughed at the expression on Greta's face.

'That is my brother, Maximilian Van Veenen. We called him Bullfrog,' he said. 'He became a movie actor, you know. At the Von Merhart studios in Schwartzgarten. He never liked me. We used to fight like cat and dog. It was Olga he liked. She was always cruel to him, but it only seemed to make him love her more.'

Greta stared at Count Sebastian in disbelief. 'Bullfrog is your brother?' It was hard to get the words out and her voice trembled as she spoke.

'Whatever is the matter?' asked Count Sebastian. 'Are you ill? Have another glass of peppermint cordial.'

Greta shook her head. 'It's Feliks,' she stammered. 'He's in grave peril.'

Count Sebastian laughed. 'Grave peril!' he exclaimed, clapping his hands in delight. 'You do have a delicious turn of phrase.'

But it was clear that Greta was talking in sober earnest.

'You don't understand,' said Greta. 'Bullfrog is in the forest. Feliks isn't safe.'

'What?' said Count Sebastian sitting bolt upright on the sofa. 'Bullfrog is here?'

Greta nodded urgently.

'He's a dangerous man,' said Count Sebastian.

'He's in the forest,' said Greta. 'Is he really very dangerous?'

'Extremely dangerous,' said Count Sebastian. 'Ludovic, telephone to the police at once!'

Count Sebastian took Greta by the hand, and together they ran out of the castle into the trees beyond.

In the village, the monsters were searching for Greta and the night sky was orange with the glow of lantern light.

'Not here,' said Doctor Kessler, trudging through the snow from the morgue.

'We've been to the very edge of the forest,' said Vladek, as he returned with Gabor. 'There was no trace of the girl.'

'Where could she have gone?' asked China Doll.

But neither Feliks nor Morbide could think what had become of Greta.

The monsters regrouped beside the frozen river.

'We'll have to travel further into the forest,' declared

Morbide. 'Greta isn't safe with wolves and black bears on the prowl.'

China Doll wrung her hands in fear.

Suddenly there was a shriek from the darkness. 'Freaks!'

A gloved hand appeared around a silver birch tree, and Olga Van Veenen emerged dressed in a hat and coat of Siberian fox fur.

'It's her!' murmured Feliks in terror.

'So here you all are,' said Olga with a devilish smile. 'Forgive me arriving unannounced and uninvited, but it seems that someone has stolen my precious angel darlings from me.'

Morbide held his great hands protectively around Feliks's shoulders. 'You're not taking them,' he growled.

'Give the children to me and I will leave you all alone,' said Olga. 'And where is little Greta? Give them to me now.'

But still Morbide would not relinquish his grip on Feliks.

'You've built a little world, have you?' said Olga with a sharp laugh, glancing around at the thatched houses of the village. 'Where no one can disturb you? Is that what you imagine?'

Doctor Kessler took a step forward, closely followed by Vladek and Gabor.

'You're going to fight me now, are you?' said Olga with a sneer.

'How did you even know the twins were here?' asked China Doll.

'Call it intuition,' replied Olga.

'Don't make me go with her,' whispered Feliks.

'You're not going anywhere,' said Morbide.

Olga snapped her fingers sharply. 'Valentin!'

Valentin stepped into the clearing, holding out his pinstriped umbrella.

'I will take back what is mine to take,' purred Olga.

'But they're not yours,' said Morbide. 'They belong here.'

'I'm touched by your obvious loyalty,' said Olga. 'But it will do you no good.'

At that moment Count Sebastian appeared through the trees with Greta.

'You're safe, Feliks!' shouted Greta in relief, not

noticing that Olga and Valentin had arrived in the village.

Before Feliks had a chance to warn his sister, Valentin seized Greta, holding the tip of his poisoned umbrella to the girl's throat.

'And you as well, Sebastian?' laughed Olga. 'Quite the little family reunion. Yes, I wondered what had become of adorable little Greta.'

'It's Bullfrog!' cried Greta. 'He's Olga's other brother. He must have told her we were here. No wonder he wanted a telephone line to connect the village to the world outside.'

Bullfrog grinned and took a step forward.

'You traitor,' screamed Greta, kicking the man sharply in the shin. 'We trusted you.'

Bullfrog howled and clutched his leg.

Karloff wheeled overhead, squawking wildly. He pecked at Valentin, who struck out violently at the bird.

'Don't you hurt him!' yelled Feliks.

'You killed the children's aunt, didn't you?' demanded Count Sebastian.

'But she had to die,' replied Olga Van Veenen. 'You

have to understand that. The children needed to be alone so I could adopt them.'

Feliks gasped and took a step backwards onto the frozen river.

'Now! Enough!' shouted Olga, following the boy onto the ice.

In desperation to protect himself, Feliks picked up a rock from the bank. He heaved the rock into the air and sent it scuddering across the ice, where it slid to a halt at Olga Van Veenen's feet. She smiled.

'Is that the best you can do?'

But as she spoke, a crack like splintering bone wiped the look of smug satisfaction from her face. Olga stared down at her feet. The ice was shattering around her shoes.

'Help me!' she screamed. But Bullfrog and Valentin were nowhere to be seen. It was too late for Olga. The ice opened beneath her, and with a desperate flailing of arms she disappeared through the icy surface of the river and was swallowed by the freezing water below.

Instinctively, Feliks took a step forward as if to help Olga, but Greta cried out, 'You'll be killed as well!'

Olga's arms reached from the water, clutching at the ice with the stiletto spikes of the cloisonné peacock. But the blade could not hold her. She slipped backwards as the spikes tore through the ice, and she was sucked down beneath the frozen surface of the river, dragged by the current. Feliks watched from the bank of the river as Olga was carried away, her head bumping up against the ice. She grasped at a rock, but it was green with algae and she could not get a grip.

'Help me!' she screamed. 'I'm drowning!'

'What can we do?' screamed Greta. 'We can't let her drown, even if she was trying to murder us.'

But there was nothing that could be done to save Olga. Still screaming, she was pulled out of sight.

'She'll be frozen to death,' said Morbide with grim certainty. 'That's the last you'll see of her.'

'Where's Valentin?' asked Feliks suddenly. 'And Bullfrog?'

Morbide shook his head.

'We must find them,' said Greta. 'We're not safe if they're on the loose.'

But there was no sign of either man. It was as if

Valentin and Bullfrog had disappeared into thin air.

'We have to get back to Schwartzgarten,' said Morbide. 'We need to tell the police the truth about Olga Van Veenen.'

'But how?' asked Feliks.

The Stationmaster shook his head. 'There isn't another train until the snow's cleared.'

'Then we shall drive back,' declared Count Sebastian. 'The snow chains will make short work of the roads. We'll travel in style!'

As the monsters packed up their possessions and prepared for their return, Count Sebastian made his way back to the castle and arranged for his fleet of gleaming Estler-Spitz motor cars to be made ready for the long journey back to Schwartzgarten.

CHAPTER TWENTY-EIGHT

Morbide was certain that once the truth of Olga's plan emerged, the monsters would be welcomed home with open arms.

Count Sebastian, who had his own suite of rooms in the Emperor Xavier Hotel, booked an adjoining suite for the twins, with a brass perch for Karloff. The monsters were to stay in a boarding house in the Old Town, also paid for by Count Sebastian.

But that night, as the twins were exploring the hotel, the Desk Clerk presented them with a carefully printed note marked:

For the eyes of the Mortenberg Twins alone.

Feliks stopped and opened the letter.

Do not trust Count Sebastian. Though he seems a friend, he is loyal only to Olga Van Veenen. Meet me at the Schwartzgarten clock tower in one hour. I have new information. Come alone. Morbide.

It seemed to the twins, as they set out from the hotel to Edvardplatz, that they could trust nobody. Only

Morbide was their loyal and constant friend.

Even from the opposite side of Edvardplatz it was apparent that a figure stood on the parapet of the tower, picked out against the illuminated clock face. As the twins drew nearer, the figure waved down at them.

'Is it Morbide?' asked Feliks, straining his eyes.

'Yes,' said Greta. 'But he's in disguise. He's wearing Duttlinger's back brace and wig.'

'But why?' asked Feliks.

'I don't know everything, do I?' snapped Greta. The cold was numbing her hands and the thought that Count Sebastian was also a traitor had rattled her nerves.

The twins turned the handle of the clock-tower door and it opened easily. Greta switched on her torch as they slowly climbed the staircase to the wooden door at the very top of the tower.

A gust of freezing air whipped through the stone chamber as Greta pushed the door open. They stepped inside and Feliks shone his torch around – until the beam settled on the grinning face of Olga Van Veenen.

'Good evening, Feliks,' said Olga, her voice chillingly polite. 'Good evening, Greta.'

Feliks croaked in horror.

'You're alive!' gasped Greta.

'It's a trap!' shouted Feliks. 'Run!'

But it was too late. The door swung shut behind them and there stood Bullfrog.

'Get them, Valentin,' shrieked Olga.

A figure appeared from the parapet; it was not Morbide at all.

'A little ruse to lure you both here,' said Olga. 'Duttlinger really should lock his shop more securely at night,' she added with a giggle.

Close up, it was clear that it was not Morbide, but Valentin dressed in the iron brace and magnetic boots that Duttlinger had designed for their friend.

'As you can see,' continued Olga, 'at a distance it is quite impossible to distinguish between Valentin and your precious Morbide.'

'What are you going to do to us?' stammered Feliks.

'I think you can guess the answer to that question, my precious boy,' said Olga. 'Valentin will hurl you both to your deaths on the cobblestones below.'

'But why?' demanded Greta. 'Everyone knows the

truth about you now. About all the other children that disappeared at Castle Van Veenen.'

'And that you killed Aunt Gisela,' shouted Feliks.

'What do you gain if you kill us as well?' said Greta.

'Satisfaction,' said Olga with a thin smile. 'It really is as simple as that.'

Bullfrog gave a rasping laugh and Valentin struck him hard on the back of the head with his metal hand.

'Quiet, Bullfrog,' he grunted.

'My name is Maximilian Van Veenen,' said Bullfrog with brooding dignity.

'Enough!' snapped Olga. 'Valentin, you know what you must do.'

Valentin attempted to take a step towards the twins in the magnetic boots; attempted, but could not. 'What's happening to me?' he spluttered.

Greta focused her torch into the corner of the chamber and the beam of light fell on the headless figure of Life, which rested against the wall.

'Removed for repairs,' said Bullfrog with a laugh. Valentin glanced down: he was standing on the moving platform that was formerly home to the headless figure.

'I read about that in *The Informant*,' continued Bullfrog. 'After all these years they're going to reattach her smiling head to her metal shoulders.'

'I don't want a history lesson,' snarled Valentin. 'I want you to help me off this thing.'

'Or else what?' said Bullfrog.

'Or else I'll throw you down onto the cobbles as well,' hissed Valentin.

He tried once more to lift his feet, but as before, he could not. The magnetic soles of Morbide's boots, hand-crafted by Duttlinger, had stuck fast to the platform. And as Valentin was practically crippled by the back brace, he was unable to bend down to free himself.

'Do something!' demanded Olga. 'This was not my plan. We need to dispose of the twins and get as far away from here as we can.'

Suddenly, the floor began to tremble. The stone chamber was alive with the sound of whirring gears and turning ratchets. Valentin felt the metal platform shake beneath him. He was moving.

'Help me, Bullfrog!' he screamed.

'MAXIMILIAN VAN VEENEN!' belched Bullfrog.

On the other side of the chamber the figure of Death had also begun to move. Bullfrog watched with amusement. Olga shrieked and struggled forward, but Bullfrog grasped her by the arms and held her back.

'I don't think so,' he giggled. 'I'm enjoying this.'

The two doors swung open onto the clock-tower parapet and there was a sudden blast of icy air.

'Goodbye, Valentin,' said Greta, smiling grimly.

Desperately, Valentin attempted to reach down to unfasten his shoelaces. But Duttlinger's back brace was so rigid that he was only able to bend slightly at the knees. On he rolled, out through the stone doorway and onto the windy parapet. With the piercing squeal of well-oiled metal, the figure of Death rolled out on its iron tracks through the opposite doorway. Valentin clutched at the walls of the tower, trying to slow his progress. But it was no good; the moving platform made a sharp movement to the right and there, facing him, was the figure of Death, its skeletal grin illuminated eerily in the orange glow of the clock face. Valentin looked down onto Edvardplatz, screaming to alert any passers-by as they crossed the cobbled square. But his voice could not be heard; the clock tower was too high, and the wind was too strong.

The twins looked from behind the metal robes of the figure of Death, as the whirring of cogs and grinding of gears sounded from inside the clock chamber. Death screeched forward on its metal wheels, jerkily raising its scythe as the mechanism ratcheted and spun. Valentin glanced around him, frantically searching for a means of escape. He gazed above him. Within grasping distance, was the hour hand of the clock. He reached up, and with a supreme effort managed to clutch hold, clawing his way upwards, still magnetically attached to the moving platform and almost lifting it from its iron track. He gasped and moaned, trying to pull himself free.

The twins watched in silence as Valentin's stockinged feet burst free from their boots: first the left foot, then the right. He snarled at the twins, pulling himself further up the hour hand towards the centre of the clock face. But just when it looked as though Valentin had escaped to safety, the clock began to strike the hour. It was a low rumble at first, growing louder and more resonant with every passing second. Powerful vibrations rattled the hands of the clock and Valentin struggled to keep his grip. As the deafening bell sounded its second chime, his fingers began to weaken their grasp, and he slipped slowly down the hour hand. The harder he tried to claw his way back up, the more he began to perspire, and the more he perspired the more slippery his remaining hand became. He slid from the clock, falling back onto the moving platform below. Held upright by the back brace, he was just in time to see Death's scythe raised high, the blade glinting in the pale moonlight.

'No!' he screamed. But it was too late. Down came the scythe. With a spurt of blood Valentin's head was swiftly and neatly separated from his neck. It tumbled from the parapet and down onto the square below, where it bounced twice and rolled around on the cobbles, before dropping into the gutter in front of the clock-tower door.

The twins hurried from the parapet to the bell chamber. There was a wrenching noise, and Death rolled backwards on its iron rails. So too did Valentin's headless corpse, still held upright by Duttlinger's remarkably effective back brace. The two figures, now both lifeless, came to a halt inside the chamber and the wooden doors of the clock tower slammed shut.

Olga Van Veenen and Bullfrog had disappeared. Pushing open Death's shuttered door, Feliks and Greta ran outside again and peered over the parapet.

'There,' said Feliks, pointing across the cobbles of Edvardplatz, in the direction of Kalvitas's chocolate shop. Two figures, a tall woman and a small man, were making good their escape.

'They're getting away,' said Greta.

Feliks watched as a constable walked close to the clock tower.

'Scream,' said Feliks. Greta turned to her brother in surprise. 'Throw back your head and scream!'

Greta did as Feliks asked. She opened her mouth wide and screamed. The constable raised his eyes to the tower and even the distant figures of Olga and Bullfrog turned to stare. Greta screamed once more, 'Catch them!'

Feliks reached over the parapet and pointed in the direction of his former guardian. The constable lifted a whistle to his lips and gave chase across Edvardplatz.

CHAPTER TWENTY-NINE

'**I**'ve got no time for evildoers,' said the Inspector of Police, as Constable Schneider led Olga Van Veenen and Bullfrog away.

'You haven't heard the last of me!' purred Olga, before the asylum wagon rattled off over the cobbles.

The Inspector smiled and his moustache twitched with satisfaction. 'She's half mad,' he observed, tapping his finger to the side of his head. 'And the other half's plain evil.'

'Well, let us hope that that is an end to that,' said Count Sebastian the next morning, pointing to the news of Olga's arrest on the front page of *The Schwartzgarten Daily Examiner.*

'You've been very kind to us,' said Greta.

Count Sebastian shook his head. 'Kindness?' he said. 'Kindness is the very least I can show you after my sister tried so determinedly to murder you both.' He reached into his waistcoat pocket and pulled out a small velvet box. He lifted the lid; inside was a golden key.

'The key,' said Count Sebastian, 'to your new home.'

Greta could feel her eyes burning.

'We don't want to live anywhere that we have to unlock with a golden key.'

Feliks sighed. 'We just want to go home,' he said. 'Home to Aunt Gisela's.'

'Climb in,' said Count Sebastian, opening the door to his Estler-Spitz. 'We're going for a spin.'

———————

Count Sebastian drove the twins across the Princess Euphenia Bridge and into the Old Town. He pulled up outside Aunt Gisela's old house.

Miserably, the twins climbed out onto the street. Count Sebastian smiled and clapped his hands. Ludovic removed the boards from the windows. Inside, the kitchen glowed just as Feliks and Greta remembered it.

'Now,' said Count Sebastian, 'put your key in the lock. Not everything is exactly as it seems.'

All of Aunt Gisela's belongings had been returned

to their former home, as if they had never been taken in the first place. But it was no longer a museum. Morbide appeared in the doorway and held out his arms to the twins.

'You are home,' he said, smiling.

———

Greta stood on a chair and hung a photograph of Aunt Gisela from a hook on the wall as Feliks opened the oven door and carefully removed a cloudberry soufflé, which had risen to perfection.

Morbide and China Doll adopted the twins and the land for a new movie studio was gifted to the monsters in perpetuity, donated by the Governor of Schwartzgarten in grateful thanks for their return to the city.

'It's ours forever,' whispered China Doll.

Morbide took her hand and nodded.

The twisted and charred wooden beams and the warped sheets of corrugated metal were cleared from the site of the Von Merhart movie studios. Morbide was invited to lay the foundation stone for the new movie studio, funded by the generosity of Count Sebastian.

The Cinema of Blood was reopened. The cockroaches were captured and moved in a crate to the insect house of the zoo.

And twice a week Greta would stand at the back of the cinema and scream.

EVER WATCHFUL

Check out more **GRUESOME**
goings-on in the city of
Schwartzgarten!

Turn the page for tonight's
late edition of

The Informant

EVER WATCHFUL

The Informant

One Curseling   Late Night Edition

VON MERHART MURDERED

– STUDIOS BURNED TO GROUND

Fritz Von Merhart, celebrated director of 'The Bloodied Handkerchief', 'The Curse of the Blind Butcher', and 'The Night of a Thousand Fangs', has himself died a bloody and unnatural death. His body was discovered early this morning, outside the Von Merhart Movie Studios, with two puncture wounds to his neck. The Department of Police have steadfastly refused to comment on rumours that the name of Von Merhart's assailant had been scrawled on the ground in the victim's own blood. It is believed that the murderer was also responsible for starting the fire that has razed the Von Merhart Movie Studios to the ground.

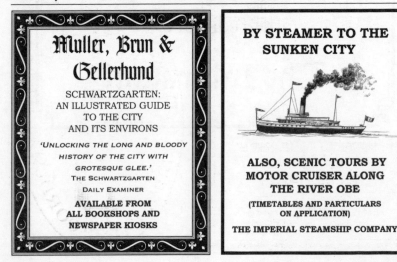

TALBOR GUILLOTINE TO BE EXHIBITED

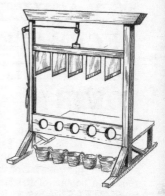

The infamous five-victim guillotine, formerly in the possession of Emeté Talbor, is to be exhibited in the Gallery of Traitors at the Governor's Palace. The violent excesses of Talbor's Reign of Terror are well documented, but words alone cannot convey the marrow-chilling awfulness of the tyrant's most notorious machine of destruction. The guillotine was designed by Talbor himself, who was quick to realise that by adding five times the number of blades to the instrument of death, he could fulfil his murderous ambitions five times as quickly. It often proved possible to behead an entire family at a single stroke. However, Talbor soon tired of this efficient way of despatching his enemies and the blades of the guillotine were deliberately blunted with the intention of decapitating his unfortunate victims as slowly and painfully as possible.

Parents of disagreeable children are reminded that the guillotine is for display only.

M. KALVITAS RECREATES IMPERIAL TORTE

Master chocolate maker M. Kalvitas has recreated the Imperial Torte that he famously invented in honour of the birth of Good Prince Eugene's only son, Wilhelm. A central tower of hazelnut sponge cake and chocolate meringue supports a marzipan replica of Prince Eugene's imperial crown, studded with gemstones of coloured sugar. Two smaller towers are topped with the crown of Princess Euphenia and the crown of the Dowager Princess, consort to Prince Alberto. The elderly chocolatier will be displaying the torte in the window of his shop on Edvardplatz to commemorate the death by firing squad of the unfortunate Prince Wilhelm.

TWO HEADS ARE INDEED PREFERABLE TO ONE

For too long Death has mocked us, grinning down at the good citizens of Schwartzgarten from the parapet of the Emperor Xavier Clock Tower. Fritz Von Merhart has been slaughtered in cold blood, and Death's painted smile grows ever wider. But Death has not always held dominion over the great city. The headless corpse of Life that stands beside the skeletal figure was once the proud owner of a serene and smiling face, which long ago tumbled from the tower, squashing to a pulp the President of the Guild of Master Locksmiths who stood on the cobbles below. Much blood was spilled that ill-fated morning and as a mark of respect to the unhappy man, the head of Life has never been replaced. But the time has surely come to remove the head from the Schwartzgarten Museum and return it to its rightful place. Life must once again restore the balance and wipe the grin from Death's cold, metal lips.

THE EDITOR

THE LILY-LIVERED PRINCE

Read on for a sneak peek of the next instalment in the

TALES FROM SCHWARTZGARTEN

…if you dare.

CHAPTER ONE

———————

IN THE depths of a cruel winter, seven families from distant lands journeyed across a strange and barren terrain. To the north there were mountains and to the south an impenetrable forest, made perilous by the presence of wolves and bears. Weary from travelling, they settled down to rest beside the river that coiled like a vast, black serpent through the frozen wasteland.

The river had frozen deep so they could not catch fish. The earth was hard as flint, so they could not dig for food.

'We must eat,' said a man, whose name was Offenbach. 'Our stomachs cry out for food, and if we do not answer that call then we shall surely die.'

The Hungry Seven, for that is how History has named the travellers, were desperate indeed. It seemed that Fate had forsaken the Seven. Cast out into the wilderness, they hoped for Life but prepared for Death.

Fate, however, is a sly master, and was not prepared to see the Hungry Seven die for want of food and warmth. As life ebbed away from the starving travellers the sky turned black with ravens, obscuring the pale winter sun with the beating of their wings. The Ravens spiralled down around the Seven bearing scraps of food, though the travellers knew not from where. The Hungry Seven felt the cold, hard beaks against their cracked lips, and they were thankful. The Ravens sheltered them with their feathers and again, the Hungry Seven were thankful.

So it was that the Seven survived that bitter winter. They survived and what is more, they prospered. As spring gave life to the land, they built simple timber buildings on the banks of the dark river. In time, the timber shacks gave way to buildings of stone and slate. As the City slowly grew, the descendants of the Hungry Seven grew ever hungrier. Though their bellies were full, they were hungry for wealth and hungry for power. And all that they wanted was theirs to have, the Ravens saw to that; the birds were protectors of the City and Guardians of the Seven. In return they sought nothing but an offering of rye bread and river water once a year at the Festival of the Departed Souls.

The names of six families of the Seven are known to all trueborn citizens of Schwartzgarten: the names of Offenbach, Koski, Engelfried, Dressler, Talbor and Van Veenen. They were illustrious and wise and strong. Their names were carved in tablets of slate that their Great Fame might live on through the generations.

But legend does not record the name of the Seventh Family. It was a cursed name that was struck from the annals of the City many centuries ago. At the head of this family was a man whom Fate had marked out for blacker deeds. His eyes were as dark as the cunning wolf and his heart was cold as granite.

'The Ravens demand too much of us,' said the one whose name is unknown. 'Our rye bread and our river water is ours to do with as we please.'

The Founding Families were in fear of the man, and bowed to his wishes, though their hearts were troubled.

When, on the eve of the Festival of the Departed Souls, the Ravens gathered to claim that which was rightfully theirs to claim, there was neither bread to eat nor water to drink. The Ravens cried a curse on the Seventh Family, which the one whose name is unknown repaid by killing seven of the birds with blade and shot and fire. It was a Dark Act indeed and the curse grew sevenfold to engulf all of the Founding Families.

The one who committed the Dark Act was cast out for his evil by the elders of each family, banished beyond the City walls and condemned to wander in shame throughout the ages. But it was not enough to undo the curse. The Ravens were protectors no more, but scavengers that spread fear and disease. Plague came and bloodshed followed. And down and down through the centuries came darkness and terror unimaginable.

———·———

The curse today has long passed, undone by the crawling passage of the years and the certain knowledge that the name of the Seventh Family is now unknowable. But what is equally certain to those that believe in such things, and is indeed recorded in the Northern Manuscripts, is this: when the Seventh of the Seven Families returns to Schwartzgarten, the Darkest of Dark Days will come once more to the Great City.

As related and translated by
Grigorius Von Hoffmeyer,
Historian and Keeper of the Northern Manuscripts

Meet Osbert Brinkhoff,
the unlikeliest of avengers.

For fans of
ROALD DAHL

THE SUNDAY TIMES
TOP SUMMER
READ 2013

OSBERT
THE AVENGER

Christopher William Hill

ISBN 9781 40831 455 5 pbk

ISBN 9781 40831 668 9 eBook